SPECIAL MESSAGE TO READERS

THE ULVERSCROFT FOUNDATION
(registered UK charity number 264873)

was established in 1972 to provide funds for
resea   es.

- •   Eye
- •   reat
- •   nd
                                                       ogy,
- •   up,
- •   rn
- •   oyal

You   on

Ev   ou
wo   r

T

**The Green, Bradgate Road, Anstey
Leicester LE7 7FU, England
Tel: (0116) 236 4325**

website: www.foundati

Agatha Christie is known throughout the world as the Queen of Crime. She is the most widely published author of all time and in any language, outsold only by the Bible and Shakespeare. Her first novel, *The Mysterious Affair at Styles*, featuring Hercule Poirot, was written towards the end of the First World War, in which she served as a VAD. She was made a Dame in 1971, and died in 1976.

The only author the Agatha Christie Estate has permitted to produce works in her name, Charles Osborne is a journalist, theatre and opera critic, poet and novelist. He unearthed, translated and adapted Oscar Wilde's previously unproduced play *Constance*, staged at The King's Head Theatre in 2011.

SPIDER'S WEB

Clarissa Hailsham-Brown, the wife of a Foreign Office diplomat, is given to day-dreaming. *Supposing I were to come down one morning and find a dead body in the library, what should I do?* She has her chance to find out when she discovers a corpse in the drawing-room of her house in Kent . . . Desperate to dispose of the body before her husband returns home accompanied by an important foreign politician, Clarissa persuades her three houseguests to become accessories and accomplices. The search begins for the murderer and the motive — all the while trying to persuade a police inspector that there has been no murder at all . . .

*Books by Agatha Christie
and Charles Osborne
Published by Ulverscroft:*

BLACK COFFEE
THE UNEXPECTED GUEST

Agatha Christie

AGATHA CHRISTIE

◆

SPIDER'S WEB

novelised by Charles Osborne

Complete and Unabridged

ULVERSCROFT
Leicester

First published in Great Britain in 2007 by
Harper
London

First Large Print Edition
published 2015
by arrangement with
HarperCollins*Publishers* Limited
London

*A catalogue record for this book is available
from the British Library.*

ISBN 978–1–4448–2612–8

Published by
F. A. Thorpe (Publishing)
Anstey, Leicestershire

Set by Words & Graphics Ltd.
Anstey, Leicestershire
Printed and bound in Great Britain by
T. J. International Ltd., Padstow, Cornwall

Foreword

It was almost certainly because of her dissatisfaction with *Alibi*, someone else's stage adaption in 1928 of her novel, *The Murder of Roger Ackroyd*, that my grandmother Agatha Christie decided to write a play of her own, which is something she had not previously attempted. *Black Coffee*, featuring her favourite detective, Hercule Poirot, was finished by the summer of 1929. But when Agatha showed it to her agent, he advised her not to bother submitting it to any theatre as, in his opinion, it was not good enough to be staged. Fortunately, a friend who was connected with theatrical management persuaded her to ignore such a negative advice, and the play was accepted for production in 1930 at the Embassy Theatre in Swiss Cottage, London.

Black Coffee was favourably received, and in April of the following year transferred to the West End, where it had a successful run of several months at the St Martin's Theatre (where a later Christie play, *The Mousetrap*, began a much longer run in 1952). In 1930, Poirot had been played by a popular actor of the time, Francis L. Sullivan, with John Boxer as his associate Captain Hastings; Joyce Bland played Lucia Amory, and Shakespearian actor Donald Wolfit was Dr Carelli. In the West End production, Francis L. Sullivan was still Poirot, but Hastings was now played by Roland Culver, and Dr Carelli by Dino Galvani.

Some months later, *Black Coffee* was filmed in England at the Twickenham Studios, directed by Leslie Hiscott and starring Austin Trevor, who had already played Poirot in the film version of *Alibi*. The play remained a favourite with repertory companies for some years, and in 1956 Charles Osborne, then earning his living as a young actor, found himself playing Dr Carelli in *Black Coffee* in a summer season at Tunbridge Wells.

Nearly forty years later, after he had in the intervening years not only become a world authority on opera but had also written a splendid book entitled *The Life and Crimes of Agatha Christie*, Osborne remembered the play. He suggested to Agatha Christie Limited (who control the copyright of her works) that, twenty years after the author's death, it would be marvellous to give the world a new Agatha Christie crime novel. We agreed enthusiastically, and the result is this Hercule Poirot murder mystery, which to me reads like authentic, vintage Christie. I feel sure Agatha would be proud to have written it.

Mathew Prichard

SPIDER'S WEB

1

Copplestone Court, the elegant, eighteenth-century country home of Henry and Clarissa Hailsham-Brown, set in gently undulating hilly country in Kent, looked handsome even at the close of a rainy March afternoon. In the tastefully furnished ground-floor drawing-room, with French windows onto the garden, two men stood near a console table on which there was a tray with three glasses of port, each marked with a sticky label, one, two and three. Also on the table was a pencil and sheet of paper.

Sir Rowland Delahaye, a distinguished-looking man in his early fifties with a charming and cultivated manner, seated himself on the arm of a comfortable chair and allowed his companion to blindfold him. Hugo Birch, a man of about sixty and inclined to be somewhat irascible in manner, then placed in Sir Rowland's hand one of the glasses from the table. Sir Rowland sipped, considered for a moment, and then said, 'I should think — yes — definitely — yes, this is the Dow 'forty-two.'

Hugo replaced the glass on the table,

murmuring 'Dow 'forty-two', made a note on the paper, and handed over the next glass. Again Sir Rowland sipped the wine. He paused, took another sip, and then nodded affirmatively. 'Ah, yes,' he declared with conviction. 'Now, this is a very fine port indeed.' He took another sip. 'No doubt about it. Cockburn 'twenty-seven.'

He handed the glass back to Hugo as he continued, 'Fancy Clarissa wasting a bottle of Cockburn 'twenty-seven on a silly experiment like this. It's positively sacrilegious. But then women just don't understand port at all.'

Hugo took the glass from him, noted his verdict on the piece of paper on the table, and handed him the third glass. After a quick sip, Sir Rowland's reaction was immediate and violent. 'Ugh!' he exclaimed in disgust. 'Rich Ruby port-type wine. I can't imagine why Clarissa has such a thing in the house.'

His opinion duly noted, he removed the blindfold. 'Now it's your turn,' he told Hugo.

Taking off his horn-rimmed spectacles, Hugo allowed Sir Rowland to blindfold him. 'Well, I imagine she uses the cheap port for jugged hare or for flavouring soup,' he suggested. 'I don't imagine Henry would allow her to offer it to guests.'

'There you are, Hugo,' Sir Rowland declared as he finished tying the blindfold

4

over his companion's eyes. 'Perhaps I ought to turn you around three times like they do in Blind Man's Buff,' he added as he led Hugo to the armchair and turned him around to sit in it.

'Here, steady on,' Hugo protested. He felt behind him for the chair.

'Got it?' asked Sir Rowland.

'Yes.'

'Then I'll swivel the glasses around instead,' Sir Rowland said as he moved the glasses on the table slightly.

'There's no need to,' Hugo told him. 'Do you think I'm likely to be influenced by what you said? I'm as good a judge of port as you are any day, Roly, my boy.'

'Don't be too sure of that. In any case, one can't be too careful,' Sir Rowland insisted.

Just as he was about to take one of the glasses across to Hugo, the third of the Hailsham-Browns' guests came in from the garden. Jeremy Warrender, an attractive young man in his twenties, was wearing a raincoat over his suit. Panting, and obviously out of breath, he headed for the sofa and was about to flop into it when he noticed what was going on. 'What on earth are you two up to?' he asked, as he removed his raincoat and jacket. 'The three-card trick with glasses?'

'What's that?' the blindfolded Hugo wanted

to know. 'It sounds as though someone's brought a dog into the room.'

'It's only young Warrender,' Sir Rowland assured him. 'Behave yourself.'

'Oh, I thought it sounded like a dog that's been chasing a rabbit,' Hugo declared.

'I've been three times to the lodge gates and back, wearing a mackintosh over my clothes,' Jeremy explained as he fell heavily onto the sofa. 'Apparently the Herzoslovakian Minister did it in four minutes fifty-three seconds, weighed down by his mackintosh. I went all out, but I couldn't do any better than six minutes ten seconds. And I don't believe he did, either. Only Chris Chataway himself could do it in that time, with or without a mackintosh.'

'Who told you that about the Herzoslovakian Minister?' Sir Rowland enquired.

'Clarissa.'

'Clarissa!' exclaimed Sir Rowland, chuckling.

'Oh, Clarissa.' Hugo snorted. 'You shouldn't pay any attention to what Clarissa tells you.'

Still chuckling, Sir Rowland continued, 'I'm afraid you don't know your hostess very well, Warrender. She's a young lady with a very vivid imagination.'

Jeremy rose to his feet. 'Do you mean she made the whole thing up?' he asked, indignantly.

'Well, I wouldn't put it past her,' Sir Rowland answered as he handed one of the three glasses to the still blindfolded Hugo. 'And it certainly sounds like her idea of a joke.'

'Does it, indeed? You just wait till I see that young woman,' Jeremy promised. 'I'll certainly have something to say to her. Gosh, I'm exhausted.' He stalked out to the hall carrying his raincoat.

'Stop puffing like a walrus,' Hugo complained. 'I'm trying to concentrate. There's a fiver at stake. Roly and I have got a bet on.'

'Oh, what is it?' Jeremy enquired, returning to perch on an arm of the sofa.

'It's to decide who's the best judge of port,' Hugo told him. 'We've got Cockburn 'twenty-seven, Dow 'forty-two, and the local grocer's special. Quiet now. This is important.' He sipped from the glass he was holding, and then murmured rather noncommittally, 'Mmm-ah.'

'Well?' Sir Roland queried. 'Have you decided what the first one is?'

'Don't hustle me, Roly,' Hugo exclaimed. 'I'm not going to rush my fences. Where's the next one?'

He held on to the glass as he was handed another. He sipped and then announced, 'Yes, I'm pretty sure about those two.' He

7

sniffed at both glasses again. 'This first one's the Dow,' he decided as he held out one glass. 'The second was the Cockburn,' he continued, handing the other glass back as Sir Rowland repeated, 'Number three glass the Dow, number one the Cockburn', writing as he spoke.

'Well, it's hardly necessary to taste the third,' Hugo declared, 'but I suppose I'd better go through with it.'

'Here you are,' said Sir Rowland, handing over the final glass.

After sipping from it, Hugo made an exclamation of extreme distaste. 'Tschah! Ugh! What unspeakable muck.' He returned the glass to Sir Rowland, then took a handkerchief from his pocket and wiped his lips to get rid of the offending taste. 'It'll take me an hour to get the taste of that stuff out of my mouth,' he complained. 'Get me out of this, Roly.'

'Here, I'll do it,' Jeremy offered, rising and moving behind Hugo to remove his blindfold while Sir Rowland thoughtfully sipped the last of the three glasses before putting it back on the table.

'So that's what you think, Hugo, is it? Glass number two, grocer's special?' He shook his head. 'Rubbish! That's the Dow 'forty-two, not a doubt of it.'

Hugo put the blindfold in his pocket. 'Pah! You've lost your palate, Roly,' he declared.

'Let me try,' Jeremy suggested. Going to the table, he took a quick sip from each glass. He paused for a moment, sipped each of them again, and then admitted, 'Well, they all taste the same to me.'

'You young people!' Hugo admonished him. 'It's all this confounded gin you keep on drinking. Completely ruins your palate. It's not just women who don't appreciate port. Nowadays, no man under forty does, either.'

Before Jeremy had a chance to reply to this, the door leading to the library opened, and Clarissa Hailsham-Brown, a beautiful dark-haired woman in her late twenties, entered. 'Hello, my darlings,' she greeted Sir Rowland and Hugo. 'Have you settled it yet?'

'Yes, Clarissa,' Sir Rowland assured her. 'We're ready for you.'

'I know I'm right,' said Hugo. 'Number one's the Cockburn, number two's the port-type stuff, and three's the Dow. Right?'

'Nonsense,' Sir Rowland exclaimed before Clarissa could answer. 'Number one's the Dow, two's the Cockburn, and three's the port-type stuff. I'm right, aren't I?'

'Darlings!' was Clarissa's only immediate response. She kissed first Hugo and then Sir Rowland, and continued, 'Now one of you

9

take the tray back to the dining-room. You'll find the decanter on the sideboard.' Smiling to herself, she selected a chocolate from a box on an occasional table.

Sir Rowland had picked up the tray with the glasses on it, and was about to leave with them. He stopped. 'The decanter?' he asked, warily.

Clarissa sat on the sofa, tucking her feet up under her. 'Yes,' she replied. 'Just one decanter.' She giggled. 'It's all the same port, you know.'

2

Clarissa's announcement produced a different reaction from each of her hearers. Jeremy burst into hoots of laughter, went across to his hostess and kissed her, while Sir Rowland stood gaping with astonishment, and Hugo seemed undecided what attitude to adopt to her having made fools of them both.

When Sir Rowland finally found words, they were, 'Clarissa, you unprincipled humbug.' But his tone was affectionate.

'Well,' Clarissa responded, 'it's been such a wet afternoon, and you weren't able to play golf. You must have some fun, and you have had fun over this, darlings, haven't you?'

'Upon my soul,' Sir Rowland exclaimed as he carried the tray to the door. 'You ought to be ashamed of yourself, showing up your elders and betters. It turns out that only young Warrender here guessed they were all the same.'

Hugo, who by now was laughing, accompanied him to the door. 'Who was it?' he asked, putting an arm around Sir Rowland's shoulder, 'Who was it who said that he'd know Cockburn 'twenty-seven anywhere?'

'Never mind, Hugo,' Sir Rowland replied resignedly, 'let's have some more of it later, whatever it is.' Talking as they went, the two men left by the door leading to the hall, Hugo closing the door behind them.

Jeremy confronted Clarissa on her sofa. 'Now then, Clarissa,' he said accusingly, 'what's all this about the Herzoslovakian Minister?'

Clarissa looked at him innocently. 'What about him?' she asked.

Pointing a finger at her, Jeremy spoke clearly and slowly. 'Did he ever run to the lodge gates and back, in a mackintosh, three times in four minutes fifty-three seconds?'

Clarissa smiled sweetly as she replied, 'The Herzoslovakian Minister is a dear, but he's well over sixty, and I doubt very much if he's run anywhere for years.'

'So you did make the whole thing up. They told me you probably did. But why?'

'Well,' Clarissa suggested, her smile even sweeter than before, 'you'd been complaining all day about not getting enough exercise. So I thought the only friendly thing to do was to help you get some. It would have been no good ordering you to go for a brisk run through the woods, but I knew you'd respond to a challenge. So I invented someone for you to challenge.'

Jeremy gave a comical groan of exasperation. 'Clarissa,' he asked her, 'do you ever speak the truth?'

'Of course I do — sometimes,' Clarissa admitted. 'But when I am speaking the truth, nobody ever seems to believe me. It's very odd.' She thought for a moment, and then continued. 'I suppose when you're making things up, you get carried away and that makes it sound more convincing.' She drifted over to the French windows.

'I might have broken a blood vessel,' Jeremy complained. 'A fat lot you'd have cared about that.'

Clarissa laughed. Opening the window she observed, 'I do believe it's cleared up. It's going to be a lovely evening. How delicious the garden smells after rain.' She leaned out and sniffed. 'Narcissus.'

As she closed the window again, Jeremy came over to join her. 'Do you really like living down here in the country?' he asked.

'I love it.'

'But you must get bored to death,' he exclaimed. 'It's all so incongruous for you, Clarissa. You must miss the theatre terribly. I hear you were passionate about it when you were younger.'

'Yes, I was. But I manage to create my own theatre right here,' said Clarissa with a laugh.

'But you ought to be leading an exciting life in London.'

Clarissa laughed again. 'What — parties and night clubs?' she asked.

'Parties, yes. You'd make a brilliant hostess,' Jeremy told her, laughing.

She turned to face him. 'It sounds like an Edwardian novel,' she said. 'Anyway, diplomatic parties are terribly dull.'

'But it's such a waste, your being tucked away down here,' he persisted, moving close to her and attempting to take her hand.

'A waste — of me?' asked Clarissa, withdrawing her hand.

'Yes,' Jeremy responded fervently. 'Then there's Henry.'

'What about Henry?' Clarissa busied herself patting a cushion on an easy chair.

Jeremy looked at her steadily. 'I can't imagine why you ever married him,' he replied, plucking up his courage. 'He's years older than you, with a daughter who's a school-kid.' He leaned on the armchair, still observing her closely. 'He's an excellent man, I have no doubt, but really, of all the pompous stuffed shirts. Going about looking like a boiled owl.' He paused, waiting for a reaction. When none came, he continued, 'He's as dull as ditchwater.'

Still she said nothing. Jeremy tried again.

'And he has no sense of humour,' he muttered somewhat petulantly.

Clarissa looked at him, smiled, but said nothing.

'I suppose you think I oughtn't to say these things,' Jeremy exclaimed.

Clarissa sat on one end of a long stool. 'Oh, I don't mind,' she told him. 'Say anything you like.'

Jeremy went over to sit beside her. 'So you do realize that you've made a mistake?' he asked, eagerly.

'But I haven't made a mistake,' was Clarissa's softly uttered response. Then, teasingly, she added, 'Are you making immoral advances to me, Jeremy?'

'Definitely,' was his prompt reply.

'How lovely,' exclaimed Clarissa. She nudged him with her elbow. 'Do go on.'

'I think you know how I feel about you, Clarissa,' Jeremy responded somewhat moodily. 'But you're just playing with me, aren't you? Flirting. It's another one of your games. Darling, can't you be serious just for once?'

'Serious? What's so good about 'serious'?' Clarissa replied. 'There's enough seriousness in the world already. I like to enjoy myself, and I like everyone around me to enjoy themselves as well.'

Jeremy smiled ruefully. 'I'd be enjoying

15

myself a great deal more at this moment if you were serious about me,' he observed.

'Oh, come on,' she ordered him playfully. 'Of course you're enjoying yourself. Here you are, our house-guest for the weekend, along with my lovely godfather Roly. And sweet old Hugo's here for drinks this evening as well. He and Roly are so funny together. You can't say you're not enjoying yourself.'

'Of course I'm enjoying myself,' Jeremy admitted. 'But you won't let me say what I really want to say to you.'

'Don't be silly, darling,' she replied. 'You know you can say anything you like to me.'

'Really? You mean that?' he asked her.

'Of course.'

'Very well, then,' said Jeremy. He rose from the stool and turned to face her. 'I love you,' he declared.

'I'm so glad,' replied Clarissa, cheerfully.

'That's entirely the wrong answer,' Jeremy complained. 'You ought to say, 'I'm so sorry' in a deep, sympathetic voice.'

'But I'm not sorry,' Clarissa insisted. 'I'm delighted. I like people to be in love with me.'

Jeremy sat down beside her again, but turned away from her. Now he seemed deeply upset. Looking at him for a moment, Clarissa asked, 'Would you do anything in the world for me?'

Turning to her, Jeremy responded eagerly. 'You know I would. Anything. Anything in the world,' he declared.

'Really?' said Clarissa. 'Supposing, for instance, that I murdered someone, would you help — no, I must stop.' She rose and walked away a few paces.

Jeremy turned to face Clarissa. 'No, go on,' he urged her.

She paused for a moment and then began to speak. 'You asked me just now if I ever got bored, down here in the country.'

'Yes.'

'Well, I suppose in a way, I do,' she admitted. 'Or, rather, I might, if it wasn't for my private hobby.'

Jeremy looked puzzled. 'Private hobby? What is that?' he asked her.

Clarissa took a deep breath. 'You see, Jeremy,' she said, 'my life has always been peaceful and happy. Nothing exciting ever happened to me, so I began to play my little game. I call it 'supposing'.'

Jeremy looked perplexed. 'Supposing?'

'Yes,' said Clarissa, beginning to pace about the room. 'For example, I might say to myself, 'Supposing I were to come down one morning and find a dead body in the library, what should I do?' Or 'Supposing a woman were to be shown in here one day and told me that she and Henry had been secretly married in Constantinople, and that our marriage was bigamous, what should I say to her?' Or 'Supposing I'd followed my instincts and become a famous actress.' Or 'Supposing I had to choose between betraying my country and seeing Henry shot before my eyes?' Do you see what I mean?' She smiled suddenly at Jeremy. 'Or even — ' She settled into the armchair. ''Supposing I were to run away with Jeremy, what would happen next?''

Jeremy went and knelt beside her. 'I feel flattered,' he told her. 'But have you ever really imagined that particular situation?'

'Oh yes,' Clarissa replied with a smile.

'Well? What did happen?' He clasped her hand.

Again she withdrew it. 'Well, the last time I played, we were on the Riviera at Juan les Pins, and Henry came after us. He had a revolver with him.'

Jeremy looked startled. 'My God!' he exclaimed. 'Did he shoot me?'

Clarissa smiled reminiscently. 'I seem to remember,' she told Jeremy, 'that he said — ' She paused, and then, adopting a highly dramatic delivery, continued, ''Clarissa, either you come back with me, or I kill myself.''

Jeremy rose and moved away. 'Jolly decent of him,' he said, sounding unconvinced. 'I can't imagine anything more unlike Henry. But, anyway, what did you say to that?'

Clarissa was still smiling complacently. 'Actually, I've played it both ways,' she admitted. 'On one occasion I told Henry that I was terribly sorry. I didn't really want him to kill himself, but I was very deeply in love with Jeremy, and there was nothing I could do about it. Henry flung himself at my feet, sobbing, but I was adamant. 'I am fond of you, Henry,' I told him, 'but I can't live without Jeremy. This is goodbye.' Then I rushed out of the house and into the garden where you were waiting for me. As we ran down the garden path to the front gate, we heard a shot ring out in the house, but we went on running.'

'Good heavens!' Jeremy gasped. 'Well, that was certainly telling him, wasn't it? Poor Henry.' He thought for a moment, and then continued, 'But you say you've played it both ways. What happened the other time?'

'Oh, Henry was so miserable, and pleaded so pitifully that I didn't have the heart to leave him. I decided to give you up, and devote my life to making Henry happy.'

Jeremy now looked absolutely desolate. 'Well, darling,' he declared ruefully, 'you certainly do have fun. But please, please be serious for a moment. I'm very serious when

I say I love you. I've loved you for a long time. You must have realized that. Are you sure there's no hope for me? Do you really want to spend the rest of your life with boring old Henry?'

Clarissa was spared from answering by the arrival of a thin, tallish child of twelve, wearing school uniform and carrying a satchel. She called out, 'Hello, Clarissa' by way of greeting as she came into the room.

'Hullo, Pippa,' her stepmother replied. 'You're late.'

Pippa put her hat and satchel on an easy chair. 'Music lesson,' she explained, laconically.

'Oh, yes,' Clarissa remembered. 'It's your piano day, isn't it? Was it interesting?'

'No. Ghastly. Awful exercises I had to repeat and repeat. Miss Farrow said it was to improve my fingering. She wouldn't let me play the nice solo piece I'd been practising. Is there any food about? I'm starving.'

Clarissa got to her feet. 'Didn't you get the usual buns to eat in the bus?' she asked.

'Oh yes,' Pippa admitted, 'but that was half an hour ago.' She gave Clarissa a pleading look that was almost comical. 'Can't I have some cake or something to last me till supper?'

Taking her hand, Clarissa led Pippa to the hall door, laughing. 'We'll see what we can find,' she promised. As they left, Pippa asked excitedly, 'Is there any of that cake left — the one with the cherries on top?'

'No,' Clarissa told her. 'You finished that off yesterday.'

Jeremy shook his head, smiling, as he heard their voices trailing away down the hall. As soon as they were out of earshot, he moved quickly to the desk and hurriedly opened one or two of the drawers. But suddenly hearing a hearty female voice calling from the garden, 'Ahoy there!', he gave a start, and hastily closed the drawers. He turned towards the French windows in time to see a big, jolly-looking woman of about forty, in tweeds and gumboots, opening the French windows. She paused as she saw Jeremy. Standing on the window step, she asked, brusquely, 'Mrs Hailsham-Brown about?'

Jeremy moved casually away from the desk, and ambled across to the sofa as he replied, 'Yes, Miss Peake. She's just gone to the kitchen with Pippa to get her something to eat. You know what a ravenous appetite Pippa always has.'

'Children shouldn't eat between meals,' was the response, delivered in ringing, almost masculine tones.

'Will you come in, Miss Peake?' Jeremy asked.

'No, I won't come in because of my boots,' she explained, with a hearty laugh. 'I'd bring half the garden with me if I did.' Again she laughed. 'I was just going to ask her what veggies she wanted for tomorrow's lunch.'

'Well, I'm afraid I — ' Jeremy began, when Miss Peake interrupted him. 'Tell you what,' she boomed, 'I'll come back.'

She began to go, but then turned back to Jeremy. 'Oh, you will be careful of that desk, won't you, Mr Warrender?' she said, peremptorily.

'Yes, of course I will,' replied Jeremy.

'It's a valuable antique, you see,' Miss Peake explained. 'You really shouldn't wrench the drawers out like that.'

Jeremy looked bemused. 'I'm terribly sorry,' he apologized. 'I was only looking for notepaper.'

'Middle pigeon-hole,' Miss Peake barked, pointing at it as she spoke.

Jeremy turned to the desk, opened the middle pigeon-hole, and extracted a sheet of writing-paper.

'That's right,' Miss Peake continued brusquely. 'Curious how often people can't see what's right in front of their eyes.' She chortled heartily as she strode away, back to the garden. Jeremy joined in her laughter, but stopped abruptly as soon as she had gone. He was about to return to the desk when Pippa came back munching a bun.

3

'Hmm. Smashing bun,' said Pippa with her mouth full, as she closed the door behind her and wiped her sticky fingers on her skirt.

'Hello, there,' Jeremy greeted her. 'How was school today?'

'Pretty foul,' Pippa responded cheerfully as she put what was left of the bun on the table. 'It was World Affairs today.' She opened her satchel. 'Miss Wilkinson loves World Affairs. But she's terribly wet. She can't keep the class in order.'

As Pippa took a book out of her satchel, Jeremy asked her, 'What's your favourite subject?'

'Biology,' was Pippa's immediate and enthusiastic answer. 'It's heaven. Yesterday we dissected a frog's leg.' She pushed her book in his face. 'Look what I got at the second-hand bookstall. It's awfully rare, I'm sure. Over a hundred years old.'

'What is it, exactly?'

'It's a kind of recipe book,' Pippa explained. She opened the book. 'It's thrilling, absolutely thrilling.'

'But what's it all about?' Jeremy wanted to know.

Pippa was already enthralled by her book. 'What?' she murmured as she turned its pages.

'It certainly seems very absorbing,' he observed.

'What?' Pippa repeated, still engrossed in the book. To herself she murmured, 'Gosh!' as she turned another page.

'Evidently a good tuppenny-worth,' Jeremy commented, and picked up a newspaper.

Apparently puzzled by what she was reading in the book, Pippa asked him, 'What's the difference between a wax candle and a tallow candle?'

Jeremy considered for a moment before replying. 'I should imagine that a tallow candle is markedly inferior,' he said. 'But surely you can't eat it? What a strange recipe book.'

Much amused, Pippa got to her feet. ''Can you eat it?'' she declaimed. 'Sounds like 'Twenty Questions'.' She laughed, threw the book onto the easy chair, and fetched a pack of cards from the bookcase. 'Do you know how to play Demon Patience?' she asked.

By now Jeremy was totally occupied with his newspaper. 'Um' was his only response.

Pippa tried again to engage his attention. 'I suppose you wouldn't like to play Beggar-my-neighbour?'

'No,' Jeremy replied firmly. He replaced the newspaper on the stool, then sat at the desk and addressed an envelope.

'No, I thought you probably wouldn't,' Pippa murmured wistfully. Kneeling on the floor in the middle of the room, she spread out her cards and began to play Demon Patience. 'I wish we could have a fine day for a change,' she complained. 'It's such a waste being in the country when it's wet.'

Jeremy looked across at her. 'Do you like living in the country, Pippa?' he asked.

'Rather,' she replied enthusiastically. 'I like it much better than living in London. This is an absolutely wizard house, with a tennis court and everything. We've even got a priest's hole.'

'A priest's hole?' Jeremy queried, smiling. 'In this house?'

'Yes, we have,' said Pippa.

'I don't believe you,' Jeremy told her. 'It's the wrong period.'

'Well, I call it a priest's hole,' she insisted. 'Look, I'll show you.'

She went to the right-hand side of the bookshelves, took out a couple of books, and pulled down a small lever in the wall behind the books. A section of wall to the right of the shelves swung open, revealing itself to be a concealed door. Behind it was a good-sized recess, with another concealed door in its back wall.

'I know it isn't really a priest's hole, of course,' Pippa admitted. 'But it's certainly a secret passage-way. Actually, that door goes through into the library.'

'Oh, does it?' said Jeremy as he went to investigate. He opened the door at the back of the recess, glanced into the library and then closed it and came back into the room. 'So it does.'

'But it's all rather secret, and you'd never guess it was there unless you knew,' Pippa said as she lifted the lever to close the panel. 'I'm using it all the time,' she continued. 'It's the sort of place that would be very convenient for putting a dead body, don't you think?'

Jeremy smiled. 'Absolutely made for it,' he agreed.

Pippa went back to her card game on the floor, as Clarissa came in.

Jeremy looked up. 'The Amazon is looking for you,' he informed her.

'Miss Peake? Oh, what a bore,' Clarissa exclaimed as she picked up Pippa's bun from the table and took a bite.

Pippa immediately got to her feet. 'Hey, that's mine!' she protested.

'Greedy thing,' Clarissa murmured as she

handed over what was left of the bun. Pippa put it back on the table and returned to her game.

'First she hailed me as though I were a ship,' Jeremy told Clarissa, 'and then she ticked me off for manhandling this desk.'

'She's a terrible pest,' Clarissa admitted, leaning over one end of the sofa to peer down at Pippa's cards. 'But we're only renting the house, and she goes with it, so — ' She broke off to say to Pippa, 'Black ten on the red Jack,' before continuing, ' — so we have to keep her on. And in any case she's really a very good gardener.'

'I know,' Jeremy agreed, putting his arm around her. 'I saw her out of my bedroom window this morning. I heard these sounds of exertion, so I stuck my head out of the window, and there was the Amazon, in the garden, digging something that looked like an enormous grave.'

'That's called deep trenching,' Clarissa explained. 'I think you plant cabbages in it, or something.'

Jeremy leaned over to study the card game on the floor. 'Red three on the black four,' he advised Pippa, who responded with a furious glare.

Emerging from the library with Hugo, Sir Rowland gave Jeremy a meaningful look. He tactfully dropped his arm and moved away from Clarissa.

'The weather seems to have cleared at last,' Sir Rowland announced. 'Too late for golf, though. Only about twenty minutes of daylight left.' Looking down at Pippa's card game, he pointed with his foot. 'Look, that goes on there,' he told her. Crossing to the French windows, he failed to notice the fierce glare Pippa shot his way. 'Well,' he said, glancing out at the garden, 'I suppose we might as well go across to the club house now, if we're going to eat there.'

'I'll go and get my coat,' Hugo announced, leaning over Pippa to point out a card as he passed her. Pippa, really furious by now, leaned forward and covered the cards with her body, as Hugo turned back to address Jeremy. 'What about you, my boy?' he asked. 'Coming with us?'

'Yes,' Jeremy answered. 'I'll just go and get my jacket.' He and Hugo went out into the hall together, leaving the door open.

'You're sure you don't mind dining at the club house this evening, darling?' Clarissa asked Sir Rowland.

'Not a bit,' he assured her. 'Very sensible arrangement, since the servants are having the night off.'

The Hailsham-Browns' middle-aged butler,

Elgin, came into the room from the hall and went across to Pippa. 'Your supper is ready in the schoolroom, Miss Pippa,' he told her. 'There's some milk, and fruit, and your favourite biscuits.'

'Oh, good!' Pippa shouted, springing to her feet. 'I'm ravenous.'

She darted towards the hall door but was stopped by Clarissa, who told her sharply to pick up her cards first and put them away.

'Oh, bother,' Pippa exclaimed. She went back to the cards, knelt, and slowly began to shovel them into a heap against one end of the sofa.

Elgin now addressed Clarissa. 'Excuse me, madam,' he murmured respectfully.

'Yes, Elgin, what is it?' Clarissa asked.

The butler looked uncomfortable. 'There has been a little — er — unpleasantness, over the vegetables,' he told her.

'Oh, dear,' said Clarissa. 'You mean with Miss Peake?'

'Yes, madam,' the butler continued. 'My wife finds Miss Peake most difficult, madam. She is continually coming into the kitchen and criticizing and making remarks, and my wife doesn't like it, she doesn't like it at all. Wherever we have been, Mrs Elgin and myself have always had very pleasant relations with the garden.'

'I'm really sorry about that,' Clarissa replied, suppressing a smile. 'I'll — er — I'll try to do something about it. I'll speak to Miss Peake.'

'Thank you, madam,' said Elgin. He bowed and left the room, closing the hall door behind him.

'How tiresome they are, servants,' Clarissa observed to Sir Rowland. 'And what curious things they say. How can one have pleasant relations with the garden? It sounds improper, in a pagan kind of way.'

'I think you're lucky, however, with this couple — the Elgins,' Sir Rowland advised her. 'Where did you get them?'

'Oh, the local Registry office,' Clarissa replied.

Sir Rowland frowned. 'I hope not that what's-its-name one where they always send you crooks,' he observed.

'Cooks?' asked Pippa, looking up from the floor where she was still sorting out cards.

'No, dear. Crooks,' Sir Rowland repeated. 'Do you remember,' he continued, now addressing Clarissa, 'that agency with the Italian or Spanish name — de Botello, wasn't it? — who kept sending you people to interview, most of whom turned out to be illegal aliens? Andy Hulme was virtually cleaned out by a couple he and his wife took on. They used Andy's horsebox to move out half the house. And they've never caught up with them yet.'

'Oh, yes,' Clarissa laughed. 'I do remember. Come on, Pippa, hurry up,' she ordered the child.

Pippa picked up the cards, and got to her feet. 'There!' she exclaimed petulantly as she replaced the cards on the bookshelves. 'I wish one didn't always have to do clearing up.' She went towards the door, but was stopped by Clarissa who, picking up what was left of Pippa's bun from the table, called to her, 'Here, take your bun with you,' and handed it to her.

Pippa started to go again. 'And your satchel,' Clarissa continued.

Pippa ran to the easy chair, snatched up her satchel, and turned again towards the hall door.

'Hat!' Clarissa shouted.

Pippa put the bun on the table, picked up her hat, and ran to the hall door.

'Here!' Clarissa called her back again, picked up the piece of bun, stuffed it in Pippa's mouth, took the hat, jammed it on the child's head, and pushed her into the hall. 'And shut the door, Pippa,' she called after her.

Pippa finally made her exit, closing the

door behind her. Sir Rowland laughed, and Clarissa, joining in, took a cigarette from a box on the table. Outside, the daylight was now beginning to fade, and the room was becoming a little darker.

'You know, it's wonderful!' Sir Rowland exclaimed. 'Pippa's a different child, now. You've done a remarkably good job there, Clarissa.'

Clarissa sank down on the sofa. 'I think she really likes me now and trusts me,' she said. 'And I quite enjoy being a stepmother.'

Sir Rowland took a lighter from the occasional table by the sofa to light Clarissa's cigarette. 'Well,' he observed, 'she certainly seems a normal, happy child again.'

Clarissa nodded in agreement. 'I think living in the country has made all the difference,' she suggested. 'And she goes to a very nice school and is making lots of friends there. Yes, I think she's happy, and, as you say, normal.'

Sir Rowland frowned. 'It's a shocking thing,' he exclaimed, 'to see a kid get into the state she was in. I'd like to wring Miranda's neck. What a dreadful mother she was.'

'Yes,' Clarissa agreed. 'Pippa was absolutely terrified of her mother.'

He joined her on the sofa. 'It was a shocking business,' he murmured.

Clarissa clenched her fists and made an

angry gesture. 'I feel furious every time I think of Miranda,' she said. 'What she made Henry suffer, and what she made that child go through. I still can't understand how any woman could.'

'Taking drugs is a nasty business,' Sir Rowland went on. 'It alters your whole character.'

They sat for a moment in silence, then Clarissa asked, 'What do you think started her on drugs in the first place?'

'I think it was her friend, that swine Oliver Costello,' Sir Rowland declared. 'I believe he's in on the drug racket.'

'He's a horrible man,' Clarissa agreed. 'Really evil, I always think.'

'She's married him now, hasn't she?'

'Yes, they married about a month ago.'

Sir Rowland shook his head. 'Well, there's no doubt Henry's well rid of Miranda,' he said. 'He's a nice fellow, Henry.' He repeated, emphatically, 'A really nice fellow.'

Clarissa smiled, and murmured gently, 'Do you think you need to tell me that?'

'I know he doesn't say much,' Sir Rowland went on. 'He's what you might call undemonstrative — but he's sound all the way through.' He paused, and then added, 'That young fellow, Jeremy. What do you know about him?'

33

Clarissa smiled again. 'Jeremy? He's very amusing,' she replied.

'Ptscha!' Sir Rowland snorted. 'That's all people seem to care about these days.' He gave Clarissa a serious look, and continued, 'You won't — you won't do anything foolish, will you?'

Clarissa laughed. 'Don't fall in love with Jeremy Warrender,' she answered him. 'That's what you mean, isn't it?'

Sir Rowland still regarded her seriously. 'Yes,' he told her, 'that's precisely what I mean. He's obviously very fond of you. Indeed, he seems unable to keep his hands off you. But you have a very happy marriage with Henry, and I wouldn't want you to do anything to put that in jeopardy.'

Clarissa gave him an affectionate smile. 'Do you really think I would do anything so foolish?' she asked, playfully.

'That would certainly be extremely foolish,' Sir Rowland advised. He paused before continuing, 'You know, Clarissa darling, I've watched you grow up. You really mean a great deal to me. If ever you're in trouble of any kind, you would come to your old guardian, wouldn't you?'

'Of course, Roly darling,' Clarissa replied. She kissed him on the cheek. 'And you needn't worry about Jeremy. Really, you needn't. I know he's very engaging, and attractive and all that. But you know me, I'm only enjoying myself. Just having fun. It's nothing serious.'

Sir Rowland was about to speak again when Miss Peake suddenly appeared at the French windows.

4

Miss Peake had by now discarded her boots, and was in her stockinged feet. She was carrying a head of broccoli.

'I hope you don't mind my coming in this way, Mrs Hailsham-Brown,' she boomed, as she strode across to the sofa. 'I shan't make the room dirty, I've left my boots outside. I'd just like you to look at this broccoli.' She thrust it belligerently over the back of the sofa and under Clarissa's nose.

'It — er — it looks very nice,' was all Clarissa could think of by way of reply.

Miss Peake pushed the broccoli at Sir Rowland. 'Take a look,' she ordered him.

Sir Rowland did as he was told and pronounced his verdict. 'I can't see anything wrong with it,' he declared. But he took the broccoli from her in order to give it a closer investigation.

'Of course there's nothing wrong with it,' Miss Peake barked at him. 'I took another one just like this into the kitchen yesterday, and that woman in the kitchen — ' She broke off to add, by way of parenthesis, 'Of course, I don't want to say anything against your servants, Mrs Hailsham-Brown, though I could say a great deal.' Returning to her main theme, she continued, 'But that Mrs Elgin actually had the nerve to tell me that it was such a poor specimen she wasn't going to cook it. She said something about, 'If you can't do better than that in the kitchen garden, you'd better take up some other job.' I was so angry I could have killed her.'

Clarissa began to speak, but Miss Peake ploughed on regardless. 'Now you know I never want to make trouble,' she insisted, 'but I'm not going into that kitchen to be insulted.' After a brief pause for breath, she resumed her tirade. 'In future,' she announced, 'I shall dump the vegetables outside the back door, and Mrs Elgin can leave a list there — '

Sir Rowland at this point attempted to hand the broccoli back to her, but Miss Peake ignored him, and continued, 'She can leave a list there of what is required.' She nodded her head emphatically.

Neither Clarissa nor Sir Rowland could think of anything to say in reply, and just as the gardener opened her mouth to speak again the telephone rang. 'I'll answer it,' she bellowed. She crossed to the phone and lifted the receiver. 'Hello — yes,' she barked into the mouthpiece, wiping the top of the table with a corner of her overall as she spoke.

'This is Copplestone Court — You want Mrs Brown? — Yes, she's here.'

Miss Peake held out the receiver, and Clarissa stubbed out her cigarette, went over to the phone, and took the receiver from her.

'Hello,' said Clarissa, 'This is Mrs Hailsham-Brown. — Hello — hello.' She looked at Miss Peake. 'How odd,' she exclaimed. 'They seem to have rung off.'

As Clarissa replaced the receiver, Miss Peake suddenly darted to the console table and set it back against the wall. 'Excuse me,' she boomed, 'but Mr Sellon always liked this table flat against the wall.'

Clarissa surreptitiously pulled a face at Sir Rowland, but hastened nevertheless to assist Miss Peake with the table. 'Thank you,' said the gardener. 'And,' she added, 'you will be careful about marks made with glasses on the furniture, won't you, Mrs Brown-Hailsham.' Clarissa looked anxiously at the table as the gardener corrected herself. 'I'm sorry — I mean Mrs Hailsham-Brown.' She laughed in a hearty fashion. 'Oh well, Brown-Hailsham, Hailsham-Brown,' she continued. 'It's really all the same thing, isn't it?'

'No, it's not, Miss Peake,' Sir Rowland declared, with very distinct enunciation. 'After all, a horse chestnut is hardly the same thing as a chestnut horse.'

While Miss Peake was laughing jovially at this, Hugo came into the room. 'Hello, there,' she greeted him. 'I'm getting a regular ticking off. Quite sarcastic, they're being.' Going across to Hugo, she thumped him on the back, and then turned to the others. 'Well, good night, all,' she shouted. 'I must be toddling back. Give me the broccoli.'

Sir Rowland handed it over. 'Horse chestnut — chestnut horse,' she boomed at him. 'Jolly good — I must remember that.' With another boisterous laugh she disappeared through the French windows.

Hugo watched her leave, and then turned to Clarissa and Sir Rowland. 'How on earth does Henry bear that woman?' he wondered aloud.

'He does actually find her very hard to take,' Clarissa replied. She picked up Pippa's book from the easy chair, put it on the table and collapsed into the chair as Hugo responded, 'I should think so. She's so damned arch! All that hearty schoolgirl manner.'

'A case of arrested development, I'm afraid,' Sir Rowland added, shaking his head.

Clarissa smiled. 'I agree she's maddening,' she said, 'but she's a very good gardener and, as I keep telling everyone, she goes with the house, and since the house is so wonderfully cheap — '

'Cheap? Is it?' Hugo interrupted her. 'You surprise me.'

'Marvellously cheap,' Clarissa told him. 'It was advertised. We came down and saw it a couple of months ago, and took it then and there for six months, furnished.'

'Whom does it belong to?' Sir Rowland asked.

'It used to belong to a Mr Sellon,' Clarissa replied. 'But he died. He was an antique dealer in Maidstone.'

'Ah, yes!' Hugo exclaimed. 'That's right. Sellon and Brown. I once bought a very nice Chippendale mirror from their shop in Maidstone. Sellon lived out here in the country, and used to go into Maidstone every day, but I believe he sometimes brought customers out here to see things that he kept in the house.'

'Mind you,' Clarissa told them both, 'there are one or two disadvantages about this house. Only yesterday, a man in a violent check suit drove up in a sports car and wanted to buy that desk.' She pointed to the desk. 'I told him that it wasn't ours and therefore we couldn't sell it, but he simply wouldn't believe me and kept on raising the price. He went up to five hundred pounds in the end.'

'Five hundred pounds!' exclaimed Sir

Rowland, sounding really startled. He went across to the desk. 'Good Lord!' he continued. 'Why, even at the Antique Dealers' Fair I wouldn't have thought it would fetch anything near to that. It's a pleasant enough object, but surely not especially valuable.'

Hugo joined him at the desk, as Pippa came back into the room. 'I'm still hungry,' she complained.

'You can't be,' Clarissa told her firmly.

'I am,' Pippa insisted. 'Milk and chocolate biscuits and a banana aren't really filling.' She made for the armchair and flung herself into it.

Sir Rowland and Hugo were still contemplating the desk. 'It's certainly a nice desk,' Sir Rowland observed. 'Quite genuine, I imagine, but not what I'd call a collector's piece. Don't you agree, Hugo?'

'Yes, but perhaps it's got a secret drawer with a diamond necklace in it,' Hugo suggested facetiously.

'It has got a secret drawer,' Pippa chimed in.

'What?' Clarissa exclaimed.

'I found a book in the market, all about secret drawers in old furniture,' Pippa explained. 'So I tried looking at desks and things all over the house. But this is the only one that's got a secret drawer.' She got up from the armchair. 'Look,' she invited them. 'I'll show you.'

She went over to the desk and opened one of its pigeonholes. While Clarissa came and leaned over the sofa to watch, Pippa slid her hand into the pigeon-hole. 'See,' she said as she did so, 'you slide this out, and there's a sort of little catch thing underneath.'

'Humph!' Hugo grunted. 'I don't call that very secret.'

'Ah, but that's not all,' Pippa went on. 'You press this thing underneath — and a little drawer flies out.' Again she demonstrated, and a small drawer shot out of the desk. 'See?'

Hugo took the drawer and picked a small piece of paper out of it. 'Hello,' he said, 'what's this, I wonder?' He read aloud. ''Sucks to you'.'

'What!' Sir Rowland exclaimed, and Pippa went off into a gale of laughter. The others joined in, and Sir Rowland playfully shook Pippa, who pretended to punch him in return as she boasted, 'I put that there!'

'You little villain!' said Sir Rowland, ruffling her hair. 'You're getting as bad as Clarissa with your silly tricks.'

'Actually,' Pippa told them, 'there was an envelope with an autograph of Queen Victoria in it. Look, I'll show you.' She dashed to the bookshelves, while Clarissa went to the desk, replaced the drawers, and closed the pigeon-hole.

At the bookshelves, Pippa opened a small box on one of the lower shelves, took out an old envelope containing three scraps of paper, and displayed them to the assembled company.

'Do you collect autographs, Pippa?' Sir Rowland asked her.

'Not really,' replied Pippa. 'Only as a side-line.' She handed one of the pieces of paper to Hugo, who glanced at it and passed it on to Sir Rowland.

'A girl at school collects stamps, and her brother's got a smashing collection himself,' Pippa told them. 'Last autumn he thought he'd got one like the one he saw in the paper — a Swedish something or other which was worth hundreds of pounds.' As she spoke, she handed the two remaining autographs and the envelope to Hugo, who passed them on to Sir Rowland.

'My friend's brother was awfully excited,' Pippa continued, 'and he took the stamp to a dealer. But the dealer said it wasn't what he thought it was, though it was quite a good stamp. Anyway, he gave him five pounds for it.'

Sir Rowland handed two of the autographs back to Hugo, who passed them on to Pippa. 'Five pounds is pretty good, isn't it?' Pippa asked him, and Hugo grunted his agreement.

Pippa looked down at the autographs. 'How much do you think Queen Victoria's autograph would be worth?' she wondered aloud.

'About five to ten shillings, I should think,' Sir Rowland told her, as he looked at the envelope he was still holding.

'There's John Ruskin's here too, and Robert Browning's,' Pippa told them.

'They're not worth much either, I'm afraid,' said Sir Rowland, handing the remaining autograph and the envelope to Hugo, who passed them on to Pippa, murmuring sympathetically as he did so, 'Sorry, my dear. You're not doing very well, are you?'

'I wish I had Neville Duke's and Roger Bannister's,' Pippa murmured wistfully. 'These historical ones are rather mouldy, I think.' She replaced the envelope and autographs in the box, placed the box back on the shelf, and then began to back towards the hall door. 'Can I see if there are any more chocolate biscuits in the larder, Clarissa?' she asked, hopefully.

'Yes, if you like,' Clarissa told her, smiling.

'We must be off,' said Hugo, following

Pippa towards the door and calling up the staircase, 'Jeremy! Hi! Jeremy!'

'Coming,' Jeremy shouted back as he hurried down the stairs carrying a golf club.

'Henry ought to be home soon,' Clarissa murmured, to herself as much as to the others.

Hugo went across to the French windows, calling to Jeremy, 'Better go out this way. It's nearer.' He turned back to Clarissa. 'Goodnight, Clarissa dear,' he said. 'Thank you for putting up with us. I'll probably go straight home from the club, but I promise to send your weekend guests back to you in one piece.'

'Goodnight, Clarissa,' Jeremy joined in, as he followed Hugo out into the garden.

Clarissa waved them goodbye, as Sir Rowland came across and put his arm around her. 'Goodnight, my dear,' he said. 'Warrender and I will probably not be in until about midnight.'

Clarissa accompanied him to the French windows. 'It's really a lovely evening,' she observed. 'I'll come with you as far as the gate onto the golf course.'

They strolled across the garden together, making no attempt to catch up with Hugo and Jeremy. 'What time do you expect Henry home?' Sir Rowland asked.

'Oh, I'm not sure. It varies. Quite soon, I imagine. Anyway, we'll have a quiet evening together and some cold food, and we'll probably have retired to bed by the time you and Jeremy get back.'

'Yes, don't wait up for us, for heaven's sake,' Sir Rowland told her.

They walked on in companionable silence until they reached the garden gate. Then, 'All right, my dear, I'll see you later, or probably at breakfast tomorrow,' said Clarissa.

Sir Rowland gave her an affectionate peck on the cheek, and walked on briskly to catch up with his companions, while Clarissa made her way back to the house. It was a pleasant evening, and she walked slowly, stopping to enjoy the sights and smells of the garden, and allowing her thoughts to wander. She laughed to herself as the image of Miss Peake with her broccoli came into her mind, then found herself smiling when she thought of Jeremy and his clumsy attempt to make love to her. She wondered idly whether he had really been serious about it. As she approached the house, she began to contemplate with pleasure the prospect of a quiet evening at home with her husband.

5

Clarissa and Sir Rowland had hardly been gone more than a few minutes when Elgin, the butler, entered the room from the hall, carrying a tray of drinks which he placed on a table. When the door bell rang, he went to the front door. A theatrically handsome, dark-haired man was standing outside.

'Good evening, sir,' Elgin greeted him.

'Good evening. I've come to see Mrs Brown,' the man told him, rather brusquely.

'Oh yes, sir, do come in,' said Elgin. Closing the door behind the man, he asked, 'What name, sir?'

'Mr Costello.'

'This way, sir.' Elgin led the way along the hall. He stood aside to allow the newcomer to enter the drawing-room, and then said, 'Would you wait here, sir. Madam is at home. I'll see if I can find her.' He started to go, then stopped and turned back to the man. 'Mr Costello, did you say?'

'That's right,' the stranger replied. 'Oliver Costello.'

'Very good, sir,' murmured Elgin as he left the room, closing the door behind him.

Left alone, Oliver Costello looked around the room, walked across to listen first at the library door and next at the hall door, and then approached the desk, bent over it, and looked closely at the drawers. Hearing a sound, he quickly moved away from the desk, and was standing in the centre of the room when Clarissa came in through the French windows.

Costello turned. When he saw who it was, he looked amazed.

It was Clarissa who spoke first. Sounding intensely surprised, she gasped, 'You?'

'Clarissa! What are you doing here?' exclaimed Costello. He sounded equally surprised.

'That's a rather silly question, isn't it?' Clarissa replied. 'It's my house.'

'This is your house?' His tone was one of disbelief.

'Don't pretend you don't know,' said Clarissa, sharply.

Costello stared at her without speaking for a moment or two. Then, adopting a complete change of manner, he observed, 'What a charming house this is. It used to belong to old what's-his-name, the antique dealer, didn't it? I remember he brought me out here once to show me some Louis Quinze chairs.' He took a cigarette case from his pocket. 'Cigarette?' he offered.

'No, thank you,' replied Clarissa abruptly. 'And,' she added, 'I think you'd better go. My husband will be home quite soon, and I don't think he'd be very pleased to see you.'

Costello responded with rather insolent amusement, 'But I particularly do want to see him. That's why I've come here, really, to discuss suitable arrangements.'

'Arrangements?' Clarissa asked, her tone one of puzzlement.

'Arrangements for Pippa,' Costello explained. 'Miranda's quite agreeable to Pippa's spending part of the summer holidays with Henry, and perhaps a week at Christmas. But otherwise — '

Clarissa interrupted him sharply. 'What do you mean?' she asked. 'Pippa's home is here.'

Costello wandered casually over to the table with the drinks on it. 'But my dear Clarissa,' he exclaimed, 'you're surely aware that the court gave Miranda the custody of the child?' He picked up a bottle of whisky. 'May I?' he asked, and without waiting for a reply poured a drink for himself. 'The case was undefended, remember?'

Clarissa faced him belligerently. 'Henry allowed Miranda to divorce him,' she declared, speaking clearly and concisely, 'only after it was agreed between them privately that Pippa should live with her father. If

49

Miranda had not agreed to that, Henry would have divorced her.'

Costello gave a laugh which bordered on a sneer. 'You don't know Miranda very well, do you?' he asked. 'She so often changes her mind.'

Clarissa turned away from him. 'I don't believe for one moment,' she said contemptuously, 'that Miranda wants that child or even cares twopence about her.'

'But you're not a mother, my dear Clarissa,' was Costello's impertinent response. 'You don't mind my calling you Clarissa, do you?' he went on, with another unpleasant smile. 'After all, now that I'm married to Miranda, we're practically relations-in-law.'

He swallowed his drink in one gulp and put his glass down. 'Yes, I can assure you,' he continued, 'Miranda is now feeling violently maternal. She feels she must have Pippa to live with us for most of the time.'

'I don't believe it,' Clarissa snapped.

'Please yourself.' Costello made himself comfortable in the armchair. 'But there's no point in your trying to contest it. After all, there was no arrangement in writing, you know.'

'You're not going to have Pippa,' Clarissa told him firmly. 'The child was a nervous wreck when she came to us. She's much better now, and she's happy at school, and that's the way she's going to remain.'

'How will you manage that, my dear?' Costello sneered. 'The law is on our side.'

'What's behind all this?' Clarissa asked him, sounding bewildered. 'You don't care about Pippa. What do you really want?' She paused, and then struck her forehead. 'Oh! What a fool I am. Of course, it's blackmail.'

Costello was about to reply, when Elgin appeared. 'I was looking for you, madam,' the butler told Clarissa. 'Will it be quite all right for Mrs Elgin and myself to leave now for the evening, madam?'

'Yes, quite all right, Elgin,' Clarissa replied.

'The taxi has come for us,' the butler explained. 'Supper is laid all ready in the dining-room.' He was about to go, but then turned back to Clarissa. 'Do you want me to shut up in here, madam?' he asked, keeping an eye on Costello as he spoke.

'No, I'll see to it,' Clarissa assured him. 'You and Mrs Elgin can go off for the evening now.'

'Thank you, madam,' said Elgin. He turned at the hall door to say, 'Goodnight, madam.'

'Goodnight, Elgin,' Clarissa responded.

Costello waited until the butler had closed the door behind him before he spoke again. 'Blackmail is a very ugly word, Clarissa,' he pointed out to her somewhat unoriginally.

'You should take a little more care before you accuse people wrongfully. Now, have I mentioned money at all?'

'Not yet,' replied Clarissa. 'But that's what you mean, isn't it?'

Costello shrugged his shoulders and held his hands out in an expressive gesture. 'It's true that we're not very well off,' he admitted. 'Miranda has always been very extravagant, as you no doubt know. I think she feels that Henry might be able to reinstate her allowance. After all, he's a rich man.'

Clarissa went up to Costello and faced him squarely. 'Now listen,' she ordered him. 'I don't know about Henry, but I do know about myself. You try to get Pippa away from here, and I'll fight you tooth and nail.' She paused, then added, 'And I don't care what weapons I use.'

Apparently unmoved by her outburst, Costello chuckled, but Clarissa continued, 'It shouldn't be difficult to get medical evidence proving Miranda's a drug addict. I'd even go to Scotland Yard and talk to the Narcotic Squad, and I'd suggest that they kept an eye on you as well.'

Costello gave a start at this. 'The upright Henry will hardly care for your methods,' he warned Clarissa.

'Then Henry will have to lump them,' she

retorted fiercely. 'It's the child that matters. I'm not going to have Pippa bullied or frightened.'

At this point, Pippa came into the room. Seeing Costello, she stopped short, looking terrified.

'Why, hello, Pippa,' Costello greeted her. 'How you've grown.'

Pippa backed away as he moved towards her. 'I've just come to make some arrangements about you,' he told her. 'Your mother is looking forward to having you with her again. She and I are married now, and — '

'I won't come,' Pippa cried hysterically, running to Clarissa for protection. 'I won't come. Clarissa, they can't make me, can they? They wouldn't — '

'Don't worry, Pippa darling,' Clarissa said soothingly, putting her arm around the child. 'Your home is here with your father and with me, and you're not leaving it.'

'But I assure you — ' Costello began, only to be interrupted angrily by Clarissa. 'Get out of here at once,' she ordered him.

Mockingly pretending to be afraid of her, Costello put his hands above his head, and backed away.

'At once!' Clarissa repeated. She advanced upon him. 'I won't have you in my house, do you hear?'

Miss Peake appeared at the French windows, carrying a large garden-fork. 'Oh, Mrs Hailsham-Brown,' she began, 'I — '

'Miss Peake,' Clarissa interrupted her. 'Will you show Mr Costello the way through the garden to the back gate?'

Costello looked at Miss Peake, who lifted her garden-fork as she returned his gaze.

'Miss — Peake?' he queried.

'Pleased to meet you,' she replied, robustly. 'I'm the gardener here.'

'Indeed, yes,' said Costello. 'I came here once before, you may remember, to look at some antique furniture.'

'Oh, yes,' Miss Peake replied. 'In Mr Sellon's time. But you can't see him today, you know. He's dead.'

'No, I didn't come to see him,' Costello declared. 'I came to see — Mrs Brown.' He gave the name a certain emphasis.

'Oh, yes? Is that so? Well, now you've seen her,' Miss Peake told him. She seemed to realize that the visitor had outstayed his welcome.

Costello turned to Clarissa. 'Goodbye, Clarissa,' he said. 'You will hear from me, you know.' He sounded almost menacing.

'This way,' Miss Peake showed him, gesturing to the French windows. She followed him out, asking as they went, 'Do you want the bus, or did you bring your own car?'

'I left my car round by the stables,' Costello informed her as they made their way across the garden.

6

As soon as Oliver Costello had left with Miss Peake, Pippa burst into tears. 'He'll take me away from here,' she cried, sobbing bitterly as she clung to Clarissa.

'No, he won't,' Clarissa assured her, but Pippa's only response was to shout, 'I hate him. I always hated him.'

Fearing that the girl was on the verge of hysteria, Clarissa addressed her sharply, 'Pippa!'

Pippa backed away from her. 'I don't want to go back to my mother, I'd rather die,' she screamed. 'I'd much rather die. I'll kill him.'

'Pippa!' Clarissa admonished her.

Pippa now seemed completely uncontrollable. 'I'll kill myself,' she cried. 'I'll cut my wrists and bleed to death.'

Clarissa seized her by the shoulders. 'Pippa, control yourself,' she ordered the child. 'It's all right, I tell you. I'm here.'

'But I don't want to go back to Mother, and I hate Oliver,' Pippa exclaimed desperately. 'He's wicked, wicked, wicked.'

'Yes, dear, I know. I know,' Clarissa murmured soothingly.

'But you don't know.' Pippa now sounded even more desperate. 'I didn't tell you everything before — when I came to live here. I just couldn't bear to mention it. But it wasn't only Miranda being so nasty and drunk or something, all the time. One night, when she was out somewhere or other, and Oliver was at home with me — I think he'd been drinking a lot — I don't know — but — ' She stopped, and for a moment seemed unable to continue. Then, forcing herself to go on, she looked down at the floor and muttered indistinctly, 'He tried to do things to me.'

Clarissa looked aghast. 'Pippa, what do you mean?' she asked. 'What are you trying to say?'

Pippa looked desperately about her, as though seeking someone else who would say the words for her. 'He — he tried to kiss me, and when I pushed him away, he grabbed me, and started to tear my dress off. Then he — ' She stopped suddenly, and burst into a fit of sobbing.

'Oh, my poor darling,' Clarissa murmured, as she hugged the child to her. 'Try not to think about it. It's all over, and nothing like that will ever happen to you again. I'll make sure that Oliver is punished for that. The disgusting beast. He won't get away with it.'

Pippa's mood suddenly changed. Her tone now had a hopeful note, as a new thought apparently came to her. 'Perhaps he'll be struck by lightning,' she wondered aloud.

'Very likely,' Clarissa agreed, 'very likely.' Her face wore a look of grim determination. 'Now pull yourself together, Pippa,' she urged the child. 'Everything's quite all right.' She took a handkerchief from her pocket. 'Here, blow your nose.'

Pippa did as she was told, and then used the handkerchief to wipe her tears off Clarissa's dress.

Clarissa managed to summon up a laugh at this. 'Now, you go upstairs and have your bath,' she ordered, turning Pippa around to face the hall door. 'Mind you have a really good wash — your neck is absolutely filthy.'

Pippa seemed to be returning to normal. 'It always is,' she replied as she went to the door. But, as she was about to leave, she turned suddenly and ran to Clarissa. 'You won't let him take me away, will you?' she pleaded.

'Over my dead body,' Clarissa replied with determination. Then she corrected herself. 'No — over *his* dead body. There! Does that satisfy you?'

Pippa nodded, and Clarissa kissed her forehead. 'Now, run along,' she ordered.

Pippa gave her stepmother a final hug, and

left. Clarissa stood for a moment in thought, and then, noticing that the room had become rather dark, switched on the concealed lighting. She went to the French windows and closed them, then sat on the sofa, staring ahead of her, apparently lost in thought.

Only a minute or two had passed when, hearing the front door of the house slam, she looked expectantly towards the hall door through which, a moment later, her husband Henry Hailsham-Brown entered. He was a quite good-looking man of about forty with a rather expressionless face, wearing horn-rimmed spectacles and carrying a briefcase.

'Hello, darling,' Henry greeted his wife, as he switched on the wall-bracket lights and put his briefcase on the armchair.

'Hello, Henry,' Clarissa replied. 'Hasn't it been an absolutely awful day?'

'Has it?' He came across to lean over the back of the sofa and kiss her.

'I hardly know where to begin,' she told him. 'Have a drink first.'

'Not just now,' Henry replied, going to the French windows and closing the curtains. 'Who's in the house?'

Slightly surprised at the question, Clarissa answered, 'Nobody. It's the Elgins' night off. Black Thursday, you know. We'll dine on cold ham, chocolate mousse, and the coffee will be really good because I shall make it.'

A questioning 'Um?' was Henry's only response to this.

Struck by his manner, Clarissa asked, 'Henry, is anything the matter?'

'Well, yes, in a way,' he told her.

'Something wrong?' she queried. 'Is it Miranda?'

'No, no, there's nothing wrong, really,' Henry assured her. 'I should say quite the contrary. Yes, quite the contrary.'

'Darling,' said Clarissa, speaking with affection and only a very faint note of ridicule, 'do I perceive behind that impenetrable Foreign Office façade a certain human excitement?'

Henry wore an air of pleasured anticipation. 'Well,' he admitted, 'it is rather exciting in a way.' He paused, then added, 'As it happens, there's a slight fog in London.'

'Is that very exciting?' Clarissa asked.

'No, no, not the fog, of course.'

'Well?' Clarissa urged him.

Henry looked quickly around, as though to assure himself that he could not be overheard, and then went across to the sofa to sit beside Clarissa. 'You'll have to keep this to yourself,' he impressed upon her, his voice very grave.

'Yes?' Clarissa prompted him, hopefully.

'It's really very secret,' Henry reiterated. 'Nobody's supposed to know. But, actually, you'll have to know.'

'Well, come on, tell me,' she urged him.

Henry looked around again, and then turned to Clarissa. 'It's all very hush-hush,' he insisted. He paused for effect, and then announced, 'The Soviet Premier, Kalendorff, is flying to London for an important conference with the Prime Minister tomorrow.'

Clarissa was unimpressed. 'Yes, I know,' she replied.

Henry looked startled. 'What do you mean, you know?' he demanded.

'I read it in the paper last Sunday,' Clarissa informed him casually.

'I can't think why you want to read these low-class papers,' Henry expostulated. He sounded really put out. 'Anyway,' he continued, 'the papers couldn't possibly know that Kalendorff was coming over. It's top secret.'

'My poor sweet,' Clarissa murmured. Then, in a voice in which compassion was mixed with incredulity, she continued, 'But top secret? Really! The things you high-ups believe.'

Henry rose and began to stride around the room, looking distinctly worried. 'Oh dear, there must have been some leak,' he muttered.

'I should have thought,' Clarissa observed tartly, 'that by now you'd know there always is a leak. In fact I should have thought that you'd all be prepared for it.'

Henry looked somewhat affronted. 'The news was only released officially tonight,' he told her. 'Kalendorff's plane is due at Heathrow at eight-forty, but actually — ' He leaned over the sofa and looked doubtfully at his wife. 'Now, Clarissa,' he asked her very solemnly, 'can I really trust you to be discreet?'

'I'm much more discreet than any Sunday newspaper,' Clarissa protested, swinging her feet off the sofa and sitting up.

Henry sat on an arm of the sofa and leaned towards Clarissa conspiratorially. 'The conference will be at Whitehall tomorrow,' he informed her, 'but it would be a great advantage if a conversation could take place first between Sir John himself and Kalendorff. Now, naturally the reporters are all waiting at Heathrow, and the moment the plane arrives Kalendorff's movements are more or less public property.'

He looked around again, as though expecting to find gentlemen of the press peering over his shoulder, and continued, in a tone of increasing excitement, 'Fortunately, this incipient fog has played into our hands.'

'Go on,' Clarissa encouraged him. 'I'm thrilled, so far.'

'At the last moment,' Henry informed her, 'the plane will find it inadvisable to land at

Heathrow. It will be diverted, as is usual on these occasions — '

'To Bindley Heath,' Clarissa interrupted him. 'That's just fifteen miles from here. I see.'

'You're always very quick, Clarissa dear,' Henry commented somewhat disapprovingly. 'But yes, I shall go off there now to the aerodrome in the car, meet Kalendorff, and bring him here. The Prime Minister is motoring down here direct from Downing Street. Half an hour will be ample for what they have to discuss, and then Kalendorff will travel up to London with Sir John.'

Henry paused. He got up and took a few paces away, before turning to say to her, disarmingly, 'You know, Clarissa, this may be of very great value to me in my career. I mean, they're reposing a lot of trust in me, having this meeting here.'

'So they should,' Clarissa replied firmly, going to her husband and flinging her arms around him. 'Henry, darling,' she exclaimed, 'I think it's all wonderful.'

'By the way,' Henry informed her solemnly, 'Kalendorff will be referred to only as Mr Jones.'

'Mr Jones?' Clarissa attempted, not altogether successfully, to keep a note of amused incredulity out of her voice.

'That's right,' Henry explained, 'one can't be too careful about using real names.'

'Yes — but — Mr Jones?' Clarissa queried. 'Couldn't they have thought of something better than that?' She shook her head doubtfully, and continued, 'Incidentally, what about me? Do I retire to the harem, as it were, or do I bring in the drinks, utter greetings to them both and then discreetly fade away?'

Henry regarded his wife somewhat uneasily as he admonished her, 'You must take this seriously, dear.'

'But Henry, darling,' Clarissa insisted, 'can't I take it seriously and still enjoy it a little?'

Henry gave her question a moment's consideration, before replying, gravely, 'I think it would be better, perhaps, Clarissa, if you didn't appear.'

Clarissa seemed not to mind this. 'All right,' she agreed, 'but what about food? Will they want something?'

'Oh no,' said Henry. 'There need be no question of a meal.'

'A few sandwiches, I think,' Clarissa suggested. She sat on an arm of the sofa, and continued, 'Ham sandwiches would be best. In a napkin to keep them moist. And hot coffee, in a Thermos jug. Yes, that'll do very well. The chocolate mousse I shall take up to my bedroom to console me for being excluded from the conference.'

'Now, Clarissa — ' Henry began, disapprovingly, only to be interrupted by his wife as she rose and flung her arms around his neck. 'Darling, I am being serious, really,' she assured him. 'Nothing will go wrong. I shan't let it.' She kissed him affectionately.

Henry gently disentangled himself from her embrace. 'What about old Roly?' he asked.

'He and Jeremy are dining at the club house with Hugo,' Clarissa told him. 'They're going to play bridge afterwards, so Roly and Jeremy won't be back here until about midnight.'

'And the Elgins are out?' Hugo asked her.

'Darling, you know they always go to the cinema on Thursdays,' Clarissa reminded him. 'They won't be back until well after eleven.'

Henry looked pleased. 'Good,' he exclaimed. 'That's all quite satisfactory. Sir John and Mr — er — '

'Jones,' Clarissa prompted him.

'Quite right, darling. Mr Jones and the Prime Minister will have left long before then.' Henry consulted his watch. 'Well, I'd better have a quick shower before I start off for Bindley Heath,' he announced.

'And I'd better go and make the ham sandwiches,' Clarissa said, dashing out of the room.

Picking up his briefcase, Henry called after her, 'You must remember about the lights, Clarissa.' He went to the door and switched off the concealed lighting. 'We're making our own electricity here, and it costs money.' He switched off the wall-brackets as well. 'It's not like London, you know.'

After a final glance around the room, which was now in darkness except for a faint glow of light from the hall door, Henry nodded and left, closing the door behind him.

7

At the golf club, Hugo was busily complaining about Clarissa's behaviour in making them test the port. 'Really, she ought to stop playing these games, you know,' he said as they made their way to the bar. 'Do you remember, Roly, the time I received that telegram from Whitehall telling me that I was going to be offered a knighthood in the next Honours List? It was only when I mentioned it in confidence to Henry one evening when I was dining with them both, and Henry was perplexed but Clarissa started giggling — it was only then that I discovered she'd sent the bloody thing. She can be so childish sometimes.'

Sir Rowland chuckled. 'Yes, she can indeed. And she loves play-acting. You know, she was actually a damned good actress in her school's drama club. At one time I thought she'd take it up seriously and go on the stage professionally. She's so convincing, even when she's telling the most dreadful lies. And that's what actors are, surely. Convincing liars.'

He was lost in reminiscence for a moment,

and then continued, 'Clarissa's best friend at school was a girl called Jeanette Collins, whose father had been a famous footballer. And Jeanette herself was a mad football fan. Well, one day Clarissa rang Jeanette in an assumed voice, claiming to be the public relations officer for some football team or other, and told her that she'd been chosen to be the team's new mascot, but that it all depended on her dressing in a funny costume as a rabbit, and standing outside the Chelsea Stadium that afternoon as the customers were queuing up to get in. Somehow Jeanette managed to hire a costume in time, and got to the stadium dressed as a bunny rabbit, where she was laughed at by hundreds of people and photographed by Clarissa who was waiting there for her. Jeanette was furious. I don't think the friendship survived.'

'Oh, well,' Hugo growled resignedly, as he picked up a menu and began to devote his attention to the serious business of choosing what they would eat later.

Meanwhile, back in the Hailsham-Browns' drawing-room, only minutes after Henry had gone off to have his shower, Oliver Costello entered the empty room stealthily through the French windows, leaving the curtains open so that moonlight streamed in. He shone a torch carefully around the room, then went to the desk and switched on the lamp that was on it. After lifting the flap of the secret drawer, he suddenly switched off the lamp and stood motionless for a moment as though he had heard something. Apparently reassured, he switched the desk lamp on again, and opened the secret drawer.

Behind Costello, the panel beside the bookshelf slowly and quietly opened. He shut the secret drawer in the desk, switched the lamp off again, and then turned sharply as he was struck a fierce blow on the head by someone standing at the recess. Costello collapsed immediately, falling behind the sofa, and the panel closed again, this time more quickly.

The room remained in darkness for a moment, until Henry Hailsham-Brown entered from the hall, switched on the wall-brackets, and shouted 'Clarissa!' Putting his spectacles on, he filled his cigarette-case from the box on a table near the sofa as Clarissa came in, calling, 'Here I am, darling. Do you want a sandwich before you go?'

'No, I think I'd better start,' Henry replied, patting his jacket nervously.

'But you'll be hours too early,' Clarissa told him. 'It can't take you more than twenty minutes to drive there.'

Henry shook his head. 'One never knows,'

he declared. 'I might have a puncture, or something might go wrong with the car.'

'Don't fuss, darling,' Clarissa admonished him, straightening his tie as she spoke. 'It's all going to go very smoothly.'

'Now, what about Pippa?' Henry asked, anxiously. 'You're sure she won't come down or barge in while Sir John and Kalen — I mean, Mr Jones, are talking privately?'

'No, there's no danger of that,' Clarissa assured him. 'I'll go up to her room and we'll have a feast together. We'll toast tomorrow's breakfast sausages and share the chocolate mousse between us.'

Henry smiled affectionately at his wife. 'You're very good to Pippa, my dear,' he told her. 'It's one of the things I'm most grateful to you for.' He paused, embarrassed, then went on. 'I can never express myself very well — I — you know — so much misery — and now, everything's so different. You — ' Taking Clarissa in his arms, he kissed her.

For some moments they remained locked in a loving embrace. Then Clarissa gently broke away, but continued to hold his hands. 'You've made me very happy, Henry,' she told him. 'And Pippa is going to be fine. She's a lovely child.'

Henry smiled affectionately at her. 'Now, you go and meet your Mr Jones,' she ordered him, pushing him towards the hall door. 'Mr Jones,' she repeated. 'I still think that's a ridiculous name to have chosen.'

Henry was about to leave the room when Clarissa asked him, 'Are you going to come in by the front door? Shall I leave it unlatched?'

He paused in the doorway to consider. Then, 'No,' he said. 'I think we'll come in through the French windows.'

'You'd better put on your overcoat, Henry. It's quite chilly,' Clarissa advised, pushing him into the hall as she spoke. 'And perhaps your muffler as well.' He took his coat obediently from a rack in the hall, and she followed him to the front door with a final word of advice. 'Drive carefully, darling, won't you?'

'Yes, yes,' Henry called back. 'You know I always do.'

Clarissa shut the door behind him, and went off to the kitchen to finish making the sandwiches. As she put them on a plate, wrapping a damp napkin around it to keep them fresh, she could not help thinking of her recent unnerving encounter with Oliver Costello. She was frowning as she carried the sandwiches back to the drawing-room, where she put them on the small table.

Suddenly fearful of incurring Miss Peake's wrath for having marked the table, she

snatched the plate up again, rubbed unsuccessfully at the mark it had made, and
compromised by covering it with a nearby
vase of flowers. She transferred the plate of
sandwiches to the stool, then carefully shook
the cushions on the sofa. Singing quietly to
herself, she picked up Pippa's book and took
it across to replace it on the bookshelves.
'Can a body meet a body, coming through
the — ' She suddenly stopped singing and
uttered a scream as she stumbled and nearly
fell over Oliver Costello.

Bending over the body, Clarissa recognized
who it was. 'Oliver!' she gasped. She stared at
him in horror for what seemed an age. Then,
convinced that he was dead, she straightened
up quickly and ran towards the door to call
Henry, but immediately realized that he had
gone. She turned back to the body, and then
ran to the telephone, and lifted the receiver.
She began to dial, but then stopped and
replaced the receiver again. She stood
thinking for a moment, and looked at the
panel in the wall. Making up her mind
quickly, she glanced at the panel again, and
then reluctantly bent down and began to drag
the body across to it.

While she was engaged in doing this, the
panel slowly opened and Pippa emerged from
the recess, wearing a dressing-gown over her

72

pyjamas. 'Clarissa!' she wailed, rushing to her stepmother.

Trying to stand between her and the body of Costello, Clarissa gave Pippa a little shove, in an attempt to turn her away. 'Pippa,' she begged, 'don't look, darling. Don't look.'

In a strangled voice, Pippa cried, 'I didn't mean to. Oh, really, I didn't mean to do it.'

Horrified, Clarissa seized the child by her arms. 'Pippa! Was it — you?' she gasped.

'He's dead, isn't he? He's quite dead?' Pippa asked. Sobbing hysterically, she cried, 'I didn't — mean to kill him. I didn't mean to.'

'Quiet now, quiet,' Clarissa murmured soothingly. 'It's all right. Come on, sit down.' She led Pippa to the armchair and sat her in it.

'I didn't mean to. I didn't mean to kill him,' Pippa went on crying.

Clarissa knelt beside her. 'Of course you didn't mean to,' she agreed. 'Now listen, Pippa — '

When Pippa continued to cry even more hysterically, Clarissa shouted at her. 'Pippa, listen to me. Everything's going to be all right. You've got to forget about this. Forget all about it, do you hear?'

'Yes,' Pippa sobbed, 'but — but I — '

'Pippa,' Clarissa continued more forcefully,

'you must trust me and believe what I'm telling you. Everything is going to be all right. But you've got to be brave and do exactly what I tell you.'

Still sobbing hysterically, Pippa tried to turn away from her.

'Pippa!' Clarissa shouted. 'Will you do as I tell you?' She pulled the child around to face her. 'Will you?'

'Yes, yes, I will,' Pippa cried, putting her head on Clarissa's bosom.

'That's right.' Clarissa adopted a consoling tone as she helped Pippa out of the chair. 'Now, I want you to go upstairs and get into bed.'

'You come with me, please,' the child pleaded.

'Yes, yes,' Clarissa assured her, 'I'll come up very soon, as soon as I can, and I'll give you a nice little white tablet. Then you'll go to sleep, and in the morning everything will seem quite different.' She looked down at the body, and added, 'There may be nothing to worry about.'

'But he is dead — isn't he?' Pippa asked.

'No, no, he may not be dead,' Clarissa replied evasively. 'I'll see. Now go on, Pippa. Do as I tell you.'

Pippa, still sobbing, left the room and ran upstairs. Clarissa watched her go, and then turned back to the body on the floor. 'Supposing I were to find a dead body in the drawing-room, what should I do?' she murmured to herself. After standing for a moment in thought, she exclaimed more emphatically, 'Oh, my God, what *am* I going to do?'

8

Fifteen minutes later, Clarissa was still in the drawing-room and murmuring to herself. But she had been busy in the meantime. All the lights were now on, the panel in the wall was closed, and the curtains had been drawn across the open French windows. Oliver Costello's body was still behind the sofa, but Clarissa had been moving the furniture about, and had set up a folding bridge-table in the centre of the room, with cards and markers for bridge, and four upright chairs around the table.

Standing at the table, Clarissa scribbled figures on one of the markers. 'Three spades, four hearts, four no trumps, pass,' she muttered, pointing at each hand as she made its call. 'Five diamonds, pass, six spades — double — and I think they go down.' She paused for a moment, looking down at the table, and then continued, 'Let me see, doubled vulnerable, two tricks, five hundred — or shall I let them make it? No.'

She was interrupted by the arrival of Sir Rowland, Hugo, and young Jeremy, who entered through the French windows. Hugo paused a moment before coming into the room, to close one half of the windows.

Putting her pad and pencil on the bridge table, Clarissa rushed to meet them. 'Thank God you've come,' she told Sir Rowland, sounding extremely distraught.

'What is all this, my dear?' Sir Rowland asked her, with concern in his voice.

Clarissa turned to address them all. 'Darlings,' she cried, 'you've got to help me.'

Jeremy noticed the table with the playing cards spread out on it. 'Looks like a bridge party,' he observed gaily.

'You're being very melodramatic, Clarissa,' Hugo contributed. 'What are you up to, young woman?'

Clarissa clutched Sir Rowland. 'It's serious,' she insisted. 'Terribly serious. You will help me, won't you?'

'Of course we'll help you, Clarissa,' Sir Rowland assured her, 'but what's it all about?'

'Yes, come on, what is it this time?' Hugo asked, somewhat wearily.

Jeremy, too, sounded unimpressed. 'You're up to something, Clarissa,' he insisted. 'What is it? Found a body or something?'

'That's just it,' Clarissa told him. 'I have — found a body.'

'What do you mean — found a body?'

Hugo asked. He sounded puzzled, but not all that interested.

'It's just as Jeremy said,' Clarissa answered him. 'I came in here, and I found a body.'

Hugo gave a cursory glance around the room. 'I don't know what you're talking about,' he complained. 'What body? Where?'

'I'm not playing games. I'm serious,' Clarissa shouted angrily. 'It's there. Go and look. Behind the sofa.' She pushed Sir Rowland towards the sofa, and moved away.

Hugo went quickly to the sofa. Jeremy followed him, and leaned over the back of it. 'My God, she's right,' Jeremy murmured.

Sir Rowland joined them. He and Hugo bent down to examine the body. 'Why, it's Oliver Costello,' Sir Rowland exclaimed.

'God almighty!' Jeremy went quickly to the French windows and drew the curtains.

'Yes,' said Clarissa. 'It's Oliver Costello.'

'What was he doing here?' Sir Rowland asked her.

'He came this evening to talk about Pippa,' Clarissa replied. 'It was just after you'd gone to the club.'

Sir Rowland looked puzzled. 'What did he want with Pippa?'

'He and Miranda were threatening to take her away,' Clarissa told him. 'But all that doesn't matter now. I'll tell you about it later.

We have to hurry. We've got very little time.'

Sir Rowland held up a hand in warning. 'Just a moment,' he instructed, coming closer to Clarissa. 'We must have the facts clear. What happened when he arrived?'

Clarissa shook her head impatiently. 'I told him that he and Miranda were not going to get Pippa, and he went away.'

'But he came back?'

'Obviously,' said Clarissa.

'How?' Sir Rowland asked her. 'When?'

'I don't know,' Clarissa answered. 'I just came into the room, as I said, and I found him — like that.' She gestured towards the sofa.

'I see,' said Sir Rowland, moving back to the body on the floor and leaning over it. 'I see. Well, he's dead all right. He's been hit over the head with something heavy and sharp.' He looked around at the others. 'I'm afraid this isn't going to be a very pleasant business,' he continued, 'but there's only one thing to be done.' He went across to the telephone as he spoke. 'We must ring up the police and — '

'No,' Clarissa exclaimed sharply.

Sir Rowland was already lifting the receiver. 'You ought to have done it at once, Clarissa,' he advised her. 'Still, I don't suppose they'll blame you much for that.'

'No, Roly, stop,' Clarissa insisted. She ran

across the room, took the receiver from him, and replaced it on its rest.

'My dear child — ' Sir Rowland expostulated, but Clarissa would not let him continue. 'I could have rung up the police myself if I'd wanted to,' she admitted. 'I knew perfectly well that it was the proper thing to do. I even started dialling. Then, instead, I rang you up at the club and asked you to come back here immediately, all three of you.' She turned to Jeremy and Hugo. 'You haven't even asked me why, yet.'

'You can leave it all to us,' Sir Rowland assured her. 'We will — '

Clarissa interrupted him vehemently. 'You haven't begun to understand,' she insisted. 'I want you to help me. You said you would if I was ever in trouble.' She turned to include the other two men. 'Darlings, you've got to help me.'

Jeremy moved to position himself so that he hid the body from her sight. 'What do you want us to do, Clarissa?' he asked gently.

'Get rid of the body,' was her abrupt reply.

'My dear, don't talk nonsense,' Sir Rowland ordered her. 'This is murder.'

'That's the whole point,' Clarissa told him. 'The body mustn't be found in this house.'

Hugo gave a snort of impatience. 'You don't know what you're talking about, my dear girl,' he exclaimed. 'You've been reading too many murder mysteries. In real life you can't go monkeying about, moving dead bodies.'

'But I've already moved it,' Clarissa explained. 'I turned it over to see if he was dead, and then I started dragging it into that recess, and then I realized I was going to need help, and so I rang you up at the club, and while I was waiting for you I made a plan.'

'Including the bridge table, I assume,' Jeremy observed, gesturing towards the table.

Clarissa picked up the bridge marker. 'Yes,' she replied. 'That's going to be our alibi.'

'What on earth — ' Hugo began, but Clarissa gave him no chance to continue. 'Two and a half rubbers,' she announced. 'I've imagined all the hands, and put down the scores on this marker. You three must fill up the others in your own handwriting, of course.'

Sir Rowland stared at her in amazement. 'You're mad, Clarissa. Quite mad,' he declared.

Clarissa paid no attention to him. 'I've worked it out beautifully,' she went on. 'The body has to be taken away from here.' She looked at Jeremy. 'It will take two of you to do that,' she instructed him. 'A dead body is very difficult to manage — I've found that out already.'

'Where the hell do you expect us to take it to?' Hugo asked in exasperation.

Clarissa had already given this some thought. 'The best place, I think, would be Marsden Wood,' she advised. 'That's only two miles from here.' She gestured away to the left. 'You turn off into that side road, just a few yards after you've passed the front gate. It's a narrow road, and there's hardly ever any traffic on it.' She turned to Sir Rowland. 'Just leave the car by the side of the road when you get into the wood,' she instructed him. 'Then you walk back here.'

Jeremy looked perplexed. 'Do you mean you want us to dump the body in the wood?' he asked.

'No, you leave it in the car,' Clarissa explained. 'It's his car, don't you see? He left it here, round by the stables.'

All three men now wore puzzled expressions. 'It's really all quite easy,' Clarissa assured them. 'If anybody does happen to see you walking back, it's quite a dark night and they won't know who you are. And you've got an alibi. All four of us have been playing bridge here.' She replaced the marker on the bridge table, looking almost pleased with herself, while the men, stupefied, stared at her.

Hugo walked about in a complete circle. 'I

— I — ' he spluttered, waving his hands in the air.

Clarissa went on issuing her instructions. 'You wear gloves, of course,' she told them, 'so as not to leave fingerprints on anything. I've got them here all ready for you.' Pushing past Jeremy to the sofa, she took three pairs of gloves from under one of the cushions, and laid them out on an arm of the sofa.

Sir Rowland continued to stare at Clarissa. 'Your natural talent for crime leaves me speechless,' he informed her.

Jeremy gazed at her admiringly. 'She's got it all worked out, hasn't she?' he declared.

'Yes,' Hugo admitted, 'but it's all damned foolish nonsense just the same.'

'Now, you must hurry,' Clarissa ordered them vehemently. 'At nine o'clock Henry and Mr Jones will be here.'

'Mr Jones? Who on earth is Mr Jones?' Sir Rowland asked her.

Clarissa put a hand to her head. 'Oh dear,' she exclaimed, 'I never realized what a terrible lot of explaining one has to do in a murder. I thought I'd simply ask you to help me and you would, and that is all there'd be to it.' She looked around at all three of them. 'Oh, darlings, you must.' She stroked Hugo's hair. 'Darling, darling Hugo — '

'This play-acting is all very well, my dear,'

83

said Hugo, sounding distinctly annoyed, 'but a dead body is a nasty, serious business, and monkeying about with it could land you in a real mess. You can't go carting bodies about at dead of night.'

Clarissa went to Jeremy and placed her hand on his arm. 'Jeremy, darling, you'll help me, surely. Won't you?' she asked, with urgent appeal in her voice.

Jeremy gazed at her adoringly. 'All right, I'm game,' he replied cheerfully. 'What's a dead body or two among friends?'

'Stop, young man,' Sir Rowland ordered. 'I'm not going to allow this.' He turned to Clarissa. 'Now, you must be guided by me, Clarissa. I insist. After all, there's Henry to consider, too.'

Clarissa gave him a look of exasperation. 'But it's Henry I *am* considering,' she declared.

9

The three men greeted Clarissa's announcement in silence. Sir Rowland shook his head gravely, Hugo continued to look puzzled, while Jeremy simply shrugged his shoulders as though giving up all hope of understanding the situation.

Taking a deep breath, Clarissa addressed all three of them. 'Something terribly important is happening tonight,' she told them. 'Henry's gone to — to meet someone and bring him back here. It's very important and secret. A top political secret. No one is supposed to know about it. There was to be absolutely no publicity.'

'Henry's gone to meet a Mr Jones?' Sir Rowland queried, dubiously.

'It's a silly name, I agree,' said Clarissa, 'but that's what they're calling him. I can't tell you his real name. I can't tell you any more about it. I promised Henry I wouldn't say a word to anybody, but I have to make you see that I'm not just — ' she turned to look at Hugo as she continued, ' — not just being an idiot and play-acting as Hugo called it.'

She turned back to Sir Rowland. 'What sort of effect do you think it will have on Henry's career,' she asked him, 'if he has to walk in here with this distinguished person — and another very distinguished person travelling down from London for this meeting — only to find the police investigating a murder — the murder of a man who has just married Henry's former wife?'

'Good Lord!' Sir Rowland exclaimed. Then, looking Clarissa straight in the eye, he added, suspiciously, 'You're not making all this up now, are you? This isn't just another of your complicated games, intended to make fools of us all?'

Clarissa shook her head mournfully. 'Nobody ever believes me when I'm speaking the truth,' she protested.

'Sorry, my dear,' said Sir Rowland. 'Yes, I can see it's a more difficult problem than I thought.'

'You see?' Clarissa urged him. 'So it's absolutely vital that we get the body away from here.'

'Where's his car, did you say?' Jeremy asked.

'Round by the stables.'

'And the servants are out, I gather?'

Clarissa nodded. 'Yes.'

Jeremy picked up a pair of gloves from the

sofa. 'Right,' he exclaimed decisively. 'Do I take the body to the car, or bring the car to the body?'

Sir Rowland held out a hand in a restraining gesture. 'Wait a moment,' he advised. 'We mustn't rush it like this.'

Jeremy put the gloves down again, but Clarissa turned to Sir Rowland, crying desperately, 'But we must hurry.'

Sir Rowland regarded her gravely. 'I'm not sure that this plan of yours is the best one, Clarissa,' he declared. 'Now, if we could just delay finding the body until tomorrow morning — that would meet the case, I think, and it would be very much simpler. If, for now, we merely moved the body to another room, for instance, I think that might be just excusable.'

Clarissa turned to address him directly. 'It's you I've got to convince, isn't it?' she told him. Looking at Jeremy, she continued, 'Jeremy's ready enough.' She glanced at Hugo. 'And Hugo will grunt and shake his head, but he'd do it all the same. It's you . . . '

She went to the library door and opened it. 'Will you both excuse us for a short time?' she asked Jeremy and Hugo. 'I want to speak to Roly alone.'

'Don't you let her talk you into any

tomfoolery, Roly,' Hugo warned as they left the room. Jeremy gave Clarissa a reassuring smile and a murmured 'Good luck!'

Sir Rowland, looking grave, took a seat at the library table.

'Now!' Clarissa exclaimed, as she sat and faced him on the other side of the table.

'My dear,' Sir Rowland warned her, 'I love you, and I will always love you dearly. But, before you ask, in this case the answer simply has to be no.'

Clarissa began to speak seriously and with emphasis. 'That man's body mustn't be found in this house,' she insisted. 'If he's found in Marsden Wood, I can say that he was here today for a short time, and I can also tell the police exactly when he left. Actually, Miss Peake saw him off, which turns out to be very fortunate. There need be no question of his ever having come back here.'

She took a deep breath. 'But if his body is found here,' she continued, 'then we shall all be questioned.' She paused before adding, with great deliberation, 'And Pippa won't be able to stand it.'

'Pippa?' Sir Rowland was obviously puzzled.

Clarissa's face was grim. 'Yes, Pippa. She'll break down and confess that she did it.'

'Pippa!' Sir Rowland repeated, as he slowly took in what he was hearing.

Clarissa nodded.

'My God!' Sir Rowland exclaimed.

'She was terrified when he came here today,' Clarissa told him. 'I tried to reassure her that I wouldn't let him take her away, but I don't think she believed me. You know what she's been through — the nervous breakdown she's had? Well, I don't think she could have survived being made to go back and live with Oliver and Miranda. Pippa was here when I found Oliver's body. She told me she never meant to do it, I'm sure she was telling the truth. It was sheer panic. She got hold of that stick, and struck out blindly.'

'What stick?' Sir Rowland asked.

'The one from the hall stand. It's in the recess. I left it there, I didn't touch it.'

Sir Rowland thought for a moment, and then asked sharply, 'Where is Pippa now?'

'In bed,' said Clarissa. 'I've given her a sleeping pill. She ought not to wake up till morning. Tomorrow I'll take her up to London, and my old nanny will look after her for a while.'

Sir Rowland got up and walked over to look down at Oliver Costello's body behind the sofa. Returning to Clarissa, he kissed her. 'You win, my dear,' he said. 'I apologize. That child musn't be asked to face the music. Get the others back.'

He went across to the window and closed it, while Clarissa opened the library door, calling, 'Hugo, Jeremy. Would you come back, please?'

The two men came back into the room. 'That butler of yours doesn't lock up very carefully,' Hugo announced. 'The window in the library was open. I've shut it now.'

Addressing Sir Rowland, he asked abruptly, 'Well?'

'I'm converted,' was the equally terse reply.

'Well done,' was Jeremy's comment.

'There's no time to lose,' Sir Rowland declared. 'Now, those gloves.' He picked up a pair and put them on. Jeremy picked up the others, handed one pair to Hugo, and they both put them on. Sir Rowland went over to the panel. 'How does this thing open?' he asked.

Jeremy went across to join him. 'Like this, sir,' he said. 'Pippa showed me.' He moved the lever and opened the panel.

Sir Rowland looked into the recess, reached in, and brought out the walking stick. 'Yes, it's heavy enough,' he commented. 'Weighted in the head. All the same, I shouldn't have thought — ' He paused.

'What wouldn't you have thought?' Hugo wanted to know.

Sir Rowland shook his head. 'I should have

thought,' he replied, 'that it would have to have been something with a sharper edge — metal of some kind.'

'You mean a goddam chopper,' Hugo observed bluntly.

'I don't know,' Jeremy interjected. 'That stick looks pretty murderous to me. You could easily crack a man's head open with that.'

'Evidently,' said Sir Rowland, drily. He turned to Hugo, and handed him the stick. 'Hugo, will you burn this in the kitchen stove, please,' he instructed. 'Warrender, you and I will get the body to the car.'

He and Jeremy bent down on either side of the body. As they did so, a bell suddenly rang. 'What's that?' Sir Rowland exclaimed, startled.

'It's the front doorbell,' said Clarissa, sounding bewildered. They all stood petrified for a moment. 'Who can it be?' Clarissa wondered aloud. 'It's much too early for Henry and — er — Mr Jones. It must be Sir John.'

'Sir John?' asked Sir Rowland, now sounding even more startled. 'You mean the Prime Minister is expected here this evening?'

'Yes,' Clarissa replied.

'Hm.' Sir Rowland looked momentarily undecided. Then, 'Yes,' he murmured. 'Well, we've got to do something.' The bell rang again, and he stirred into action. 'Clarissa,' he ordered, 'go and answer the door. Use whatever delaying tactics you can think of. In the meantime, we'll clear up in here.'

Clarissa went quickly out to the hall, and Sir Rowland turned to Hugo and Jeremy. 'Now then,' he explained urgently, 'this is what we do. We'll get him into that recess. Later, when everyone's in this room having their pow-wow, we can take him out through the library.'

'Good idea,' Jeremy agreed, as he helped Sir Rowland lift the body.

'Want me to give you a hand?' asked Hugo.

'No, it's all right,' Jeremy replied. He and Sir Rowland supported Costello's body under the armpits and carried it into the recess, while Hugo picked up the torch. A moment or two later, Sir Rowland emerged and pressed the lever as Jeremy hastened out behind him. Hugo quickly slipped under Jeremy's arm into the recess with the torch and stick. The panel then closed.

Sir Rowland, after examining his jacket for signs of blood, murmured, 'Gloves,' removed the gloves he was wearing, and put them under a cushion on the sofa. Jeremy removed his gloves and did likewise. Then, 'Bridge,' Sir Rowland reminded himself, as he hastened to the bridge table and sat.

Jeremy followed him and picked up his

cards. 'Come along, Hugo, make haste,' Sir Rowland urged as he picked up his own cards.

He was answered by a knock from inside the recess. Suddenly realizing that Hugo was not in the room, Sir Rowland and Jeremy looked at each other in alarm. Jeremy got up, rushed to the switch and opened the panel. 'Come along, Hugo,' Sir Rowland repeated urgently, as Hugo emerged. 'Quickly, Hugo,' Jeremy muttered impatiently, closing the panel again.

Sir Rowland took Hugo's gloves from him, and put them under the cushion. The three men took their seats quickly at the bridge table and picked up their cards, just as Clarissa came back into the room from the hall, followed by two men in uniform.

In a tone of innocent surprise, Clarissa announced, 'It's the police, Uncle Roly.'

10

The older of the two police officers, a stocky, grey-haired man, followed Clarissa into the room, while his colleague remained standing by the hall door. 'This is Inspector Lord,' Clarissa declared. 'And — ' she turned back to the younger officer, a dark-haired man in his twenties with the build of a footballer. 'I'm sorry, what did you say your name was?' she asked.

The Inspector answered for him. 'That's Constable Jones,' he announced. Addressing the three men, he continued, 'I'm sorry to intrude, gentlemen, but we have received information that a murder has been committed here.'

Clarissa and her friends all spoke simultaneously. 'What?' Hugo shouted. 'A murder!' Jeremy exclaimed. 'Good heavens,' Sir Rowland cried, as Clarissa said, 'Isn't it extraordinary?' They all sounded completely astonished.

'Yes, we had a telephone call at the station,' the Inspector told them. Nodding to Hugo, he added, 'Good evening, Mr Birch.'

'Er — good evening, Inspector,' Hugo mumbled.

'It looks as though somebody's been hoaxing you, Inspector,' Sir Rowland suggested.

'Yes,' Clarissa agreed. 'We've been playing bridge here all evening.'

The others nodded in support, and Clarissa asked, 'Who did they say had been murdered?'

'No names were mentioned,' the Inspector informed them. 'The caller just said that a man had been murdered at Copplestone Court, and would we come along immediately. They rang off before any additional information could be obtained.'

'It must have been a hoax,' Clarissa declared, adding virtuously, 'What a wicked thing to do.'

Hugo tut-tutted, and the Inspector replied, 'You'd be surprised, madam, at the potty things people do.'

He paused, glancing at each of them in turn, and then continued, addressing Clarissa. 'Well now, according to you, nothing out of the ordinary has happened here this evening?' Without waiting for an answer, he added, 'Perhaps I'd better see Mr Hailsham-Brown as well.'

'He's not here,' Clarissa told the Inspector. 'I don't expect him back until late tonight.'

'I see,' he replied. 'Who is staying in the house at present?'

'Sir Rowland Delahaye, and Mr Warrender,' said Clarissa, indicating them in turn. She added, 'And Mr Birch, whom you already know, is here for the evening.'

Sir Rowland and Jeremy murmured acknowledgements. 'Oh, and yes,' Clarissa went on as though she had just remembered, 'my little stepdaughter.' She emphasized 'little'. 'She's in bed and asleep.'

'What about servants?' the Inspector wanted to know.

'There are two of them. A married couple. But it's their night out, and they've gone to the cinema in Maidstone.'

'I see,' said the Inspector, nodding his head gravely.

Just at that moment, Elgin came into the room from the hall, almost colliding with the Constable who was still keeping guard there. After a quick questioning look at the Inspector, Elgin addressed Clarissa. 'Would you be wanting anything, madam?' he asked.

Clarissa looked startled. 'I thought you were at the pictures, Elgin,' she exclaimed, as the Inspector gave her a sharp glance.

'We returned almost immediately, madam,' Elgin explained. 'My wife was not feeling well.' Sounding embarrassed, he added, delicately, 'Er — gastric trouble. It must have been something she ate.' Looking from the

Inspector to the Constable, he asked, 'Is anything — wrong?'

'What's your name?' the Inspector asked him.

'Elgin, sir,' the butler replied. 'I'm sure I hope there's nothing — '

He was interrupted by the Inspector. 'Someone rang up the police station and said that a murder had been committed here.'

'A murder?' Elgin gasped.

'What do you know about that?'

'Nothing. Nothing at all, sir.'

'It wasn't you who rang up, then?' the Inspector asked him.

'No, indeed not.'

'When you returned to the house, you came in by the back door — at least I suppose you did?'

'Yes, sir,' Elgin replied, nervousness now making him rather more deferential in manner.

'Did you notice anything unusual?'

The butler thought for a moment, and then replied, 'Now I come to think of it, there was a strange car standing near the stables.'

'A strange car? What do you mean?'

'I wondered at the time whose it might be,' Elgin recalled. 'It seemed a curious place to leave it.'

'Was there anybody in it?'

'Not so far as I could see, sir.'

'Go and take a look at it, Jones,' the Inspector ordered his Constable.

'Jones!' Clarissa exclaimed involuntarily, with a start.

'I beg your pardon?' said the Inspector, turning to her.

Clarissa recovered herself quickly. Smiling at him, she murmured, 'It's nothing — just — I didn't think he looked very Welsh.'

The Inspector gestured to Constable Jones and to Elgin, indicating that they should go. They left the room together, and a silence ensued. After a moment, Jeremy moved to sit on the sofa and began to eat the sandwiches. The Inspector put his hat and gloves on the armchair, and then, taking a deep breath, addressed the assembled company.

'It seems,' he declared, speaking slowly and deliberately, 'that someone came here tonight who is unaccounted for.' He looked at Clarissa. 'You're sure you weren't expecting anyone?' he asked her.

'Oh, no — no,' Clarissa replied. 'We didn't want anyone to turn up. You see, we were just the four of us for bridge.'

'Really?' said the Inspector. 'I'm fond of a game of bridge myself.'

'Oh, are you?' Clarissa replied. 'Do you play Blackwood?'

'I just like a common-sense game,' the Inspector told her. 'Tell me, Mrs Hailsham-Brown,' he continued, 'you haven't lived here for very long, have you?'

'No,' she told him. 'About six weeks.'

The Inspector regarded her steadily. 'And there's been no funny business of any kind since you've been living here?' he asked.

Before Clarissa could answer, Sir Rowland interjected. 'What exactly do you mean by funny business, Inspector?'

The Inspector turned to address him. 'Well, it's rather a curious story, sir,' he informed Sir Rowland. 'This house used to belong to Mr Sellon, the antique dealer. He died six months ago.'

'Yes,' Clarissa remembered. 'He had some kind of accident, didn't he?'

'That's right,' said the Inspector. 'He fell downstairs, pitched on his head.' He looked around at Jeremy and Hugo, and added, 'Accidental death, they brought in. It might have been that, but it might not.'

'Do you mean,' Clarissa asked, 'that somebody might have pushed him?'

The Inspector turned to her. 'That,' he agreed, 'or else somebody hit him a crack on the head — '

He paused, and the tension among his hearers was palpable. Into the silence the

Inspector went on. 'Someone could have arranged Sellon's body to look right, at the bottom of the stairs.'

'The staircase here in this house?' Clarissa asked nervously.

'No, it happened at his shop,' the Inspector informed her. 'There was no conclusive evidence, of course — but he was rather a dark horse, Mr Sellon.'

'In what way, Inspector?' Sir Rowland asked him.

'Well,' the Inspector replied, 'once or twice there were a couple of things he had to explain to us, as you might say. And the Narcotics Squad came down from London and had a word with him on one occasion . . . ' He paused before continuing, 'but it was all no more than suspicion.'

'Officially, that is to say,' Sir Rowland observed.

The Inspector turned to him. 'That's right, sir,' he said meaningfully. 'Officially.'

'Whereas, unofficially — ?' Sir Rowland prompted him.

'I'm afraid we can't go into that,' the Inspector replied. He went on, 'There was, however, one rather curious circumstance. There was an unfinished letter on Mr Sellon's desk, in which he mentioned that he'd come into possession of something which he described as an unparalleled rarity, which he would — ' Here the Inspector paused, as if recollecting the exact words, ' — would guarantee wasn't a forgery, and he was asking fourteen thousand pounds for it.'

Sir Rowland looked thoughtful. 'Fourteen thousand pounds,' he murmured. In a louder voice he continued, 'Yes, that's a lot of money indeed. Now, I wonder what it could be? Jewellery, I suppose, but the word forgery suggests — I don't know, a picture, perhaps?'

Jeremy continued to munch at the sandwiches, as the Inspector replied, 'Yes, perhaps. There was nothing in the shop worth such a large sum of money. The insurance inventory made that clear. Mr Sellon's partner was a woman who has a business of her own in London, and she wrote and said she couldn't give us any help or information.'

Sir Rowland nodded his head slowly. 'So he might have been murdered, and the article, whatever it was, stolen,' he suggested.

'It's quite possible, sir,' the Inspector agreed, 'but again, the would-be thief may not have been able to find it.'

'Now, why do you think that?' Sir Rowland asked.

'Because,' the Inspector replied, 'the shop has been broken into twice since then. Broken into and ransacked.'

Clarissa looked puzzled. 'Why are you telling us all this, Inspector?' she wanted to know.

'Because, Mrs Hailsham-Brown,' said the Inspector, turning to her, 'it's occurred to me that whatever was hidden away by Mr Sellon may have been hidden here in this house, and not at his shop in Maidstone. That's why I asked you if anything peculiar had come to your notice.'

Holding up a hand as though she had suddenly remembered, Clarissa said excitedly, 'Somebody rang up only today and asked to speak to me, and when I came to the phone whoever it was had just hung up. In a way, that's rather odd, isn't it?' She turned to Jeremy, adding, 'Oh yes, of course. You know, that man who came the other day and wanted to buy things — a horsey sort of man in a check suit. He wanted to buy that desk.'

The Inspector crossed the room to look at the desk. 'This one here?' he asked.

'Yes,' Clarissa replied. 'I told him, of course, that it wasn't ours to sell, but he didn't seem to believe me. He offered me a large sum, far more than it's worth.'

'That's very interesting,' the Inspector commented as he studied the desk. 'These things often have a secret drawer, you know.'

'Yes, this one has,' Clarissa told him. 'But

there was nothing very exciting in it. Only some old autographs.'

The Inspector looked interested. 'Old autographs can be immensely valuable, I understand,' he said. 'Whose were they?'

'I can assure you, Inspector,' Sir Rowland informed him, 'that these weren't anything rare enough to be worth more than a pound or two.'

The door to the hall opened, and Constable Jones entered, carrying a small booklet and a pair of gloves.

'Yes, Jones? What is it?' the Inspector asked him.

'I've examined the car, sir,' he replied. 'Just a pair of gloves on the driving seat. But I found this registration book in the side pocket.' He handed the book to the Inspector, and Clarissa exchanged a smile with Jeremy as they heard the Constable's strong Welsh accent.

The Inspector examined the registration book. ''Oliver Costello, 27 Morgan Mansions, London SW3',' he read aloud. Then, turning to Clarissa, he asked sharply, 'Has a man called Costello been here today?'

11

The four friends exchanged guiltily furtive glances. Clarissa and Sir Rowland both looked as though they were about to attempt an answer, but it was Clarissa who actually spoke. 'Yes,' she admitted. 'He was here about — ' She paused, and then, 'let me see,' she continued. 'Yes, it was about half past six.'

'Is he a friend of yours?' the Inspector asked her.

'No, I wouldn't call him a friend,' Clarissa replied. 'I had met him only once or twice.' She deliberately assumed an embarrassed look, and then said, hesitantly, 'It's — a little awkward, really — ' She looked appealingly at Sir Rowland, as though passing the ball to him.

That gentleman was quick to respond to her unspoken request. 'Perhaps, Inspector,' he said, 'it would be better if I explained the situation.'

'Please do, sir,' the Inspector responded somewhat tersely.

'Well,' Sir Rowland continued, 'it concerns the first Mrs Hailsham-Brown. She and

Hailsham-Brown were divorced just over a year ago, and recently she married Mr Oliver Costello.'

'I see,' observed the Inspector. 'And Mr Costello came here today.' He turned to Clarissa. 'Why was that?' he asked. 'Did he come by appointment?'

'Oh no,' Clarissa replied glibly. 'As a matter of fact, when Miranda and my husband divorced, she took with her one or two things that weren't really hers. Oliver Costello happened to be in this part of the world, and he just looked in to return them to Henry.'

'What kind of things?' the Inspector asked quickly.

Clarissa was ready for this question. 'Nothing very important,' she said with a smile. Picking up the small silver cigarette-box from a table by the sofa, she held it out to the Inspector. 'This was one of them,' she told him. 'It belonged to my husband's mother, and he values it for sentimental reasons.'

The Inspector looked at Clarissa reflectively for a moment, before asking her, 'How long did Mr Costello remain here when he came at six-thirty?'

'Oh, a very short time,' she replied as she replaced the cigarette box on the table. 'He said he was in a hurry. About ten minutes, I should think. No longer than that.'

'And your interview was quite amicable?' the Inspector enquired.

'Oh, yes,' Clarissa assured him. 'I thought it was very kind of him to take the trouble to return the things.'

The Inspector thought for a moment, before asking, 'Did he mention where he was going when he left here?'

'No,' Clarissa replied. 'Actually, he went out by that window,' she continued, gesturing towards the French windows. 'As a matter of fact, my lady gardener, Miss Peake, was here, and she offered to show him out through the garden.'

'Your gardener — does she live on the premises?' the Inspector wanted to know.

'Well, yes. But not in the house. She lives in the cottage.'

'I think I should like a word with her,' the Inspector decided. He turned to the Constable. 'Jones, go and get her.'

'There's a telephone connection through to the cottage. Shall I call her for you, Inspector?' Clarissa offered.

'If you would be so kind, Mrs Hailsham-Brown,' the Inspector replied.

'Not at all. I don't suppose she'll have gone to bed yet,' Clarissa said, pressing a button on the telephone. She flashed a smile at the

Inspector, who responded by looking bashful. Jeremy smiled to himself and took another sandwich.

Clarissa spoke into the telephone. 'Hello, Miss Peake. This is Mrs Hailsham-Brown . . . I wonder, would you mind coming over? Something rather important has happened . . . Oh yes, of course that will be all right. Thank you.'

She replaced the receiver and turned to the Inspector. 'Miss Peake has been washing her hair, but she'll get dressed and come right over.'

'Thank you,' said the Inspector. 'After all, Costello may have mentioned to her where he was going.'

'Yes, indeed, he may have,' Clarissa agreed.

The Inspector looked puzzled. 'The question that bothers me,' he announced to the room in general, 'is why Mr Costello's car is still here, and where is Mr Costello?'

Clarissa gave an involuntary glance towards the bookshelves and the panel, then walked across to the French windows to watch for Miss Peake. Jeremy, noticing her glance, sat back innocently and crossed his legs as the Inspector continued, 'Apparently this Miss Peake was the last person to see him. He left, you say, by that window. Did you lock it after him?'

'No,' Clarissa replied, standing at the window with her back to the Inspector.

'Oh?' the Inspector queried.

Something in his tone made Clarissa turn to face him. 'Well, I — I don't think so,' she said, hesitantly.

'So he might have re-entered that way,' the Inspector observed. He took a deep breath and announced importantly, 'I think, Mrs Hailsham-Brown, that, with your permission, I should like to search the house.'

'Of course,' Clarissa replied with a friendly smile. 'Well, you've seen this room. Nobody could be hidden here.' She held the window curtains open for a moment, as though awaiting Miss Peake, and then exclaimed, 'Look! Through here is the library.' Going to the library door and opening it, she suggested, 'Would you like to go in there?'

'Thank you,' said the Inspector. 'Jones!' As the two police officers went into the library, the Inspector added, 'Just see where that door leads to, Jones,' gesturing towards another door immediately inside the library.

'Very good, sir,' the Constable replied, as he went through the door indicated.

As soon as they were out of earshot, Sir Rowland went to Clarissa. 'What's on the other side?' he asked her quietly, indicating the panel.

'Bookshelves,' she replied tersely.

He nodded and strolled nonchalantly across to the sofa, as the Constable's voice was heard calling, 'Just another door through to the hall, sir.'

The two officers returned from the library. 'Right,' said the Inspector. He looked at Sir Rowland, apparently taking note of the fact that he had moved. 'Now we'll search the rest of the house,' he announced, going to the hall door.

'I'll come with you, if you don't mind,' Clarissa offered, 'in case my little stepdaughter should wake up and be frightened. Not that I think she will. It's extraordinary how deeply children can sleep. You have to practically shake them awake.'

As the Inspector opened the hall door, she asked him, 'Have you got any children, Inspector?'

'One boy and one girl,' he replied shortly, as he made his way out of the room, crossed the hall, and began to ascend the stairs.

'Isn't that nice?' Clarissa observed. She turned to the Constable. 'Mr Jones,' she invited him with a gesture to precede her. He made his way out of the room and she followed him closely.

As soon as they had gone, the three remaining occupants of the room looked at one another. Hugo wiped his hands and Jeremy mopped his forehead. 'And now what?' Jeremy asked, taking another sandwich.

Sir Rowland shook his head. 'I don't like this,' he told them. 'We're getting in very deep.'

'If you ask me,' Hugo advised him, 'there's only one thing to do. Come clean. Own up now before it's too late.'

'Damn it, we can't do that,' Jeremy exclaimed. 'It would be too unfair to Clarissa.'

'But we'll get her in a worse mess if we keep on with this,' Hugo insisted. 'How are we ever going to get the body away? The police will impound the fellow's car.'

'We could use mine,' Jeremy suggested.

'Well, I don't like it,' Hugo persisted. 'I don't like it at all. Damn it, I'm a local JP. I've got my reputation with the police here to consider.' He turned to Sir Rowland. 'What do you say, Roly? You've got a good level head.'

Sir Rowland looked grave. 'I admit I don't like it,' he replied, 'but personally I am committed to the enterprise.'

Hugo looked perplexed. 'I don't understand you,' he told his friend.

'Take it on trust, if you will, Hugo,' said Sir

Rowland. He looked gravely at both men, and continued, 'We're in a very bad jam, all of us. But if we stick together and have reasonable luck, I think there's a chance we may be able to pull it off.'

Jeremy looked as though he was about to say something, but Sir Rowland held up a hand, and went on, 'Once the police are satisfied that Costello isn't in this house, they'll go off and look elsewhere. After all, there are plenty of reasons why he might have left his car and gone off on foot.' He gestured towards them both and added, 'We're all respectable people — Hugo's a JP, as he's reminded us, and Henry Hailsham-Brown's high up in the Foreign Office — '

'Yes, yes, and you've had a blameless and even distinguished career, we know all that,' Hugo intervened. 'All right then, if you say so, we brazen it out.'

Jeremy rose to his feet and nodded towards the recess. 'Can't we do something about that straightaway?' he asked.

'There's no time now,' Sir Rowland decreed, tersely. 'They'll be back any minute. He's safer where he is.'

Jeremy nodded in reluctant agreement. 'I must say Clarissa's a marvel,' he observed. 'She doesn't turn a hair. She's got that police inspector eating out of her hand.'

111

The front door bell rang. 'That'll be Miss Peake, I expect,' Sir Rowland announced. 'Go and let her in, Warrender, would you?'

As soon as Jeremy had left the room, Hugo beckoned to Sir Rowland.

'What's up, Roly?' he asked in an urgent whisper. 'What did Clarissa tell you when she got you to herself?'

Sir Rowland began to speak, but, hearing the voices of Jeremy and Miss Peake exchanging greetings at the front door, he made a gesture indicating 'Not now'.

'I think you'd better come in here,' Jeremy told Miss Peake as he slammed the front door shut. A moment later, the gardener preceded him into the drawing-room, looking as though she had dressed very hastily. She had a towel wrapped around her head.

'What is all this?' she wanted to know. 'Mrs Hailsham-Brown was most mysterious on the phone. Has anything happened?'

Sir Rowland addressed her with the utmost courtesy. 'I'm so sorry you've been routed out like this, Miss Peake,' he apologized. 'Do sit down.' He indicated a chair by the bridge table.

Hugo pulled the chair out for Miss Peake, who thanked him. He then seated himself in a more comfortable easy chair, while Sir Rowland informed the gardener, 'As a matter of fact, we've got the police here, and — '

'The police?' Miss Peake interrupted, looking startled. 'Has there been a burglary?'

'No, not a burglary, but — '

He stopped speaking as Clarissa, the Inspector and the Constable came back into the room. Jeremy sat on the sofa, while Sir Rowland took up a position behind it.

'Inspector,' Clarissa announced, 'this is Miss Peake.'

The Inspector went across to the gardener. His 'Good evening, Miss Peake' was accompanied by a stiff little bow.

'Good evening, Inspector,' Miss Peake replied. 'I was just asking Sir Rowland — has there been a robbery, or what?'

The Inspector regarded her searchingly, allowed a moment or two to elapse, and then spoke. 'We received a rather peculiar telephone call which brought us out here,' he told her. 'And we think that perhaps you might be able to clear up the matter for us.'

12

The Inspector's announcement was greeted by Miss Peake with a jolly laugh. 'I say, this is mysterious. I *am* enjoying myself,' she exclaimed delightedly.

The Inspector frowned. 'It concerns Mr Costello,' he explained. 'Mr Oliver Costello of 27, Morgan Mansions, London SW3. I believe that's in the Chelsea area.'

'Never heard of him,' was Miss Peake's robustly expressed response.

'He was here this evening, visiting Mrs Hailsham-Brown,' the Inspector reminded her, 'and I believe you showed him out through the garden.'

Miss Peake slapped her thigh. 'Oh, that man,' she recalled. 'Mrs Hailsham-Brown did mention his name.' She looked at the Inspector with a little more interest. 'Yes, what do you want to know?' she asked.

'I should like to know,' the Inspector told her, speaking slowly and deliberately, 'exactly what happened, and when you last saw him.'

Miss Peake thought for a moment before replying. 'Let me see,' she said. 'We went out through the French window, and I told him there was a short cut if he wanted the bus, and he said no, he'd come in his car, and he'd left it round by the stables.'

She beamed at the Inspector as though she expected to be praised for her succinct recollection of what had occurred, but he merely looked thoughtful as he commented, 'Isn't that rather an odd place to leave a car?'

'That's just what I thought,' Miss Peake agreed, slapping the Inspector's arm as she spoke. He looked surprised at this, but she continued, 'You'd think he'd drive right up to the front door, wouldn't you? But people are so odd. You never know what they're going to do.' She gave a hearty guffaw.

'And then what happened?' the Inspector asked.

Miss Peake shrugged her shoulders. 'Well, he went off to his car, and I suppose he drove away,' she replied.

'You didn't see him do so?'

'No — I was putting my tools away,' was the gardener's reply.

'And that's the last you saw of him?' the Inspector asked, with emphasis.

'Yes, why?'

'Because his car is still here,' the Inspector told her. Speaking slowly and emphatically, he continued, 'A phone-call was put through to the police station at seven forty-nine,

115

saying that a man had been murdered at Copplestone Court.'

Miss Peake looked appalled. 'Murdered?' she exclaimed. 'Here? Ridiculous!'

'That's what everybody seems to think,' the Inspector observed drily, with a significant look at Sir Rowland.

'Of course,' Miss Peake went on, 'I know there are all these maniacs about, attacking women — but you say a man was murdered — '

The Inspector cut her short. 'You didn't hear another car this evening?' he asked brusquely.

'Only Mr Hailsham-Brown's,' she replied.

'Mr Hailsham-Brown?' the Inspector queried with a raise of his eyebrows. 'I thought he wasn't expected home till late.'

His glance swung round to Clarissa, who hastened to explain. 'My husband did come home, but he had to go out again almost immediately.'

The Inspector assumed a deliberately patient expression. 'Oh, is that so?' he commented in a tone of studied politeness. 'Exactly when did he come home?'

'Let me see — ' Clarissa began to stammer. 'It must have been about — '

'It was about a quarter of an hour before I went off duty,' Miss Peake interjected. 'I work

116

a lot of overtime, Inspector. I never stick to regulation hours,' she explained. 'Be keen on your job, that's what I say,' she continued, thumping the table as she spoke. 'Yes, it must have been about a quarter past seven when Mr Hailsham-Brown got in.'

'That would have been shortly after Mr Costello left,' the Inspector observed. He moved to the centre of the room, and his manner changed almost imperceptibly as he continued, 'He and Mr Hailsham-Brown probably passed each other.'

'You mean,' Miss Peake said thoughtfully, 'that he may have come back again to see Mr Hailsham-Brown.'

'Oliver Costello definitely didn't come back to the house,' Clarissa cut in sharply.

'But you can't be sure of that, Mrs Hailsham-Brown,' the gardener contradicted her. 'He might have got in by that window without your knowing anything about it.' She paused, and then exclaimed, 'Golly! You don't think he murdered Mr Hailsham-Brown, do you? I say, I am sorry.'

'Of course he didn't murder Henry,' Clarissa snapped irritably.

'Where did your husband go when he left here?' the Inspector asked her.

'I've no idea,' Clarissa replied shortly.

'Doesn't he usually tell you where he's

going?' the Inspector persisted.

'I never ask questions,' Clarissa told him. 'I think it must be so boring for a man if his wife is always asking questions.'

Miss Peake gave a sudden squeal. 'But how stupid of me,' she shouted. 'Of course, if that man's car is still here, then he must be the one who's been murdered.' She roared with laughter.

Sir Rowland rose to his feet. 'We've no reason to believe anyone has been murdered, Miss Peake,' he admonished her with dignity. 'In fact, the Inspector believes it was all some silly hoax.'

Miss Peake was clearly not of the same opinion. 'But the car,' she insisted. 'I do think that car still being here is very suspicious.' She got up and approached the Inspector. 'Have you looked about for the body, Inspector?' she asked him eagerly.

'The Inspector has already searched the house,' Sir Rowland answered before the police officer had a chance to speak. He was rewarded by a sharp glance from the Inspector, whom Miss Peake was now tapping on the shoulder as she continued to air her views.

'I'm sure those Elgins have something to do with it — the butler and that wife of his who calls herself a cook,' the gardener assured the Inspector confidently. 'I've had my suspicions of them for quite some time. I saw a light in their bedroom window as I came along here just now. And that in itself is suspicious. It's their night out, and they usually don't return until well after eleven.' She gripped the Inspector's arm. 'Have you searched their quarters?' she asked him urgently.

The Inspector opened his mouth to speak, but she interrupted him with another tap on the shoulder. 'Now listen,' she began. 'Suppose this Mr Costello recognized Elgin as a man with a criminal record. Costello might have decided to come back and warn Mrs Hailsham-Brown about the man, and Elgin assaulted him.'

Looking immensely pleased with herself, she flashed a glance around the room, and continued. 'Then, of course, Elgin would have to hide the body somewhere quickly, so that he could dispose of it later in the night. Now, where would he hide it, I wonder?' she asked rhetorically, warming to her thesis. With a gesture towards the French windows, she began, 'Behind a curtain or — '

She was cut short by Clarissa who interrupted angrily. 'Oh, really, Miss Peake. There isn't anybody hidden behind any of the curtains. And I'm sure Elgin would never murder anybody. It's quite ridiculous.'

Miss Peake turned. 'You're so trusting, Mrs Hailsham-Brown,' she admonished her employer. 'When you get to my age, you'll realize how very often people are simply not quite what they seem.' She laughed heartily as she turned back to the Inspector.

When he opened his mouth to speak, she gave him yet another tap on the shoulder. 'Now then,' she continued, 'where would a man like Elgin hide the body? There's that cupboard place between here and the library. You've looked there, I suppose?'

Sir Rowland intervened hastily. 'Miss Peake, the Inspector has looked both here *and* in the library,' he insisted.

The Inspector, however, after a meaningful look at Sir Rowland, turned to the gardener. 'What exactly do you mean by 'that cupboard place', Miss Peake?' he enquired.

The others in the room all looked more than somewhat tense as Miss Peake replied, 'Oh, it's a wonderful place when you're playing hide-and-seek. You'd really never dream it was there. Let me show it to you.'

She walked over to the panel, followed by the Inspector. Jeremy got to his feet at the same moment that Clarissa exclaimed forcefully, 'No.'

The Inspector and Miss Peake both turned to look at her. 'There's nothing there now,'

Clarissa informed them. 'I know because I went that way, through to the library, just now.'

Her voice trailed off. Miss Peake, sounding disappointed, murmured, 'Oh well, in that case, then — ' and turned away from the panel. The Inspector, however, called her back. 'Just show me all the same, Miss Peake,' he ordered. 'I'd like to see.'

Miss Peake went to the bookshelves. 'It was a door originally,' she explained. 'It matched the one over there.' She activated the lever, explaining as she did so, 'You pull this catch back, and the door comes open. See?'

The panel opened, and the body of Oliver Costello slumped down and fell forward. Miss Peake screamed.

'So,' the Inspector observed, looking grimly at Clarissa, 'You were mistaken, Mrs Hailsham-Brown. It appears that there was a murder here tonight.'

Miss Peake's scream rose to a crescendo.

13

Ten minutes later, things were somewhat quieter, for Miss Peake was no longer in the room. Nor, for that matter, were Hugo and Jeremy. The body of Oliver Costello, however, was still lying collapsed in the recess, the panel of which was open. Clarissa was stretched out on the sofa, with Sir Rowland sitting by her and holding a glass of brandy which he was attempting to make her sip. The Inspector was talking on the telephone, and Constable Jones continued to stand guard.

'Yes, yes — ' the Inspector was saying. 'What's that? — Hit and run? — Where? — Oh, I see — Yes, well, send them along as soon as you can — Yes, we'll want photographs — Yes, the whole bag of tricks.'

He replaced the receiver, and went over to the Constable. 'Everything comes at once,' he complained to his colleague. 'Weeks go by and nothing happens, and now the Divisional Surgeon's out at a bad car accident — a smash on the London road. It'll all mean quite a bit of delay. However, we'll get on as well as we can until the M.O. arrives.' He gestured towards the corpse. 'We'd better not move him until they've taken the photographs,' he suggested. 'Not that it will tell us anything. He wasn't killed there, he was put there afterwards.'

'How can you be sure, sir?' the Constable asked.

The Inspector looked down at the carpet. 'You can see where his feet have dragged,' he pointed out, crouching down behind the sofa. The Constable knelt beside him.

Sir Rowland peered over the back of the sofa, and then turned to Clarissa to ask, 'How are you feeling now?'

'Better, thanks, Roly,' she replied, faintly.

The two police officers got to their feet. 'It might be as well to close that book-case door,' the Inspector instructed his colleague. 'We don't want any more hysterics.'

'Right, sir,' the Constable replied. He closed the panel so that the body could no longer be seen. As he did so, Sir Rowland rose from the sofa to address the Inspector. 'Mrs Hailsham-Brown has had a bad shock,' he told the policeman. 'I think she ought to go to her room and lie down.'

Politely, but with a certain reserve, the Inspector replied, 'Certainly, sir, but not for a moment or two just yet. I'd like to ask her a few questions first.'

Sir Rowland tried to persist. 'She's really

not fit to be questioned at present.'

'I'm all right, Roly,' Clarissa interjected, faintly. 'Really, I am.'

Sir Rowland addressed her, adopting a warning tone. 'It's very brave of you, my dear,' he said, 'but I really think it would be wiser of you to go and rest for a while.'

'Dear Uncle Roly,' Clarissa responded with a smile. To the Inspector she said, 'I sometimes call him Uncle Roly, though he's my guardian, not my uncle. But he's so sweet to me always.'

'Yes, I can see that,' was the dry response.

'Do ask me anything you want to, Inspector,' Clarissa continued graciously. 'Though actually I don't think I can help you very much, I'm afraid, because I just don't know anything at all about any of this.'

Sir Rowland sighed, shook his head slightly, and turned away.

'We shan't worry you for long, madam,' the Inspector assured her. Going to the library door, he held it open, and turned to address Sir Rowland. 'Will you join the other gentlemen in the library, sir?' he suggested.

'I think I'd better remain here, in case — ' Sir Rowland began, only to be interrupted by the Inspector whose tone had now become firmer. 'I'll call you if it should be necessary, sir. In the library, please.'

After a short duel of eyes, Sir Rowland conceded defeat and went into the library. The Inspector closed the door after him, and indicated silently to the Constable that he should sit and take notes. Clarissa swung her feet off the sofa and sat up, as Jones got out his notebook and pencil.

'Now, Mrs Hailsham-Brown,' the Inspector began, 'if you're ready, let's make a start.' He picked up the cigarette box from the table by the sofa, turned it over, opened it, and looked at the cigarettes in it.

'Dear Uncle Roly, he always wants to spare me everything,' Clarissa told the Inspector with an enchanting smile. Then, seeing him handling the cigarette box, she became anxious. 'This isn't going to be the third degree or anything, is it?' she asked, trying to make her question sound like a joke.

'Nothing of that kind, madam, I assure you,' said the Inspector. 'Just a few simple questions.' He turned to the Constable. 'Are you ready, Jones?' he asked, as he pulled out a chair from the bridge table, turned it around, and sat facing Clarissa.

'All ready, sir,' Constable Jones replied.

'Good. Now, Mrs Hailsham-Brown,' the Inspector began. 'Do you say that you had no idea there was a body concealed in that recess?'

The Constable began his note-taking as Clarissa answered, wide-eyed, 'No, of course not. It's horrible.' She shivered. 'Quite horrible.'

The Inspector looked at her enquiringly. 'When we were searching this room,' he asked, 'why didn't you call our attention to that recess?'

Clarissa met his gaze with a look of wide-eyed innocence. 'Do you know,' she said, 'the thought never struck me. You see, we never use the recess, so it just didn't come into my head.'

The Inspector pounced. 'But you said,' he reminded her, 'that you had just been through there into the library.'

'Oh no,' Clarissa exclaimed quickly. 'You must have misunderstood me.' She pointed to the library door. 'What I meant was that we had gone through that door into the library.'

'Yes, I certainly must have misunderstood you,' the Inspector observed grimly. 'Now, let me at least be clear about this. You say you have no idea when Mr Costello came back to this house, or what he might have come for?'

'No, I simply can't imagine,' Clarissa replied, her voice dripping with innocent candour.

'But the fact remains that he did come back,' the Inspector persisted.

'Yes, of course. We know that now.'

'Well, he must have had some reason,' the Inspector pointed out.

'I suppose so,' Clarissa agreed. 'But I've no idea what it could have been.'

The Inspector thought for a moment, and then tried another line of approach. 'Do you think that perhaps he wanted to see your husband?' he suggested.

'Oh, no,' Clarissa replied quickly, 'I'm quite sure he didn't. Henry and he never liked each other.'

'Oh!' the Inspector exclaimed. 'They never liked each other. I didn't realize that. Had there been a quarrel between them?'

Again Clarissa spoke quickly to forestall a new and potentially dangerous line of enquiry. 'Oh no,' she assured the Inspector, 'no, they hadn't quarrelled. Henry just thought he wore the wrong shoes.' She smiled engagingly. 'You know how odd men can be.'

The Inspector's look suggested that this was something of which he was personally ignorant. 'You're absolutely certain that Costello wouldn't have come back here to see you?' he asked again.

'Me?' Clarissa echoed innocently. 'Oh no, I'm sure he didn't. What reason could he possibly have?'

The Inspector took a deep breath. Then,

speaking slowly and deliberately, he asked her, 'Is there anybody else in the house he might have wanted to see? Now please think carefully before you answer.'

Again, Clarissa gave him her look of bland innocence. 'I can't think who,' she insisted. 'I mean, who else is there?'

The Inspector rose, turned his chair around and put it back against the bridge table. Then, pacing slowly about the room, he began to muse. 'Mr Costello comes here,' he began slowly, 'and returns the articles which the first Mrs Hailsham-Brown had taken from your husband by mistake. Then he says good-bye. But then he comes back to the house.'

He went across to the French windows. 'Presumably he effects an entrance through these windows,' he continued, gesturing at them. 'He is killed — and his body is pushed into that recess — all in a space of about ten to twenty minutes.'

He turned back to face Clarissa. 'And nobody hears anything?' he ended, on a rising inflection. 'I find that very difficult to believe.'

'I know,' Clarissa agreed. 'I find it just as difficult to believe. It's really extraordinary, isn't it?'

'It certainly is,' the Inspector agreed, his tone distinctly ironical. He tried one last time. 'Mrs Hailsham-Brown, are you absolutely sure that you didn't hear anything?' he asked her pointedly.

'I heard nothing at all,' she answered. 'It really is fantastic.'

'Almost too fantastic,' the Inspector commented grimly. He paused, then went over to the hall door and held it open. 'Well, that's all for the present, Mrs Hailsham-Brown.'

Clarissa rose and walked rather quickly towards the library door, only to be intercepted by the Inspector. 'Not that way, please,' he instructed her, and led her over to the hall door.

'But I think, really, I'd rather join the others,' she protested.

'Later, if you don't mind,' said the Inspector tersely.

Very reluctantly, Clarissa went out through the hall door.

14

The Inspector closed the hall door behind Clarissa, then went over to Constable Jones who was still writing in his notebook. 'Where's the other woman? The gardener. Miss — er — Peake?' the Inspector asked.

'I put her on the bed in the spare room,' the Constable told his superior. 'After she came out of the hysterics, that is. A terrible time I had with her, laughing and crying something terrible, she was.'

'It doesn't matter if Mrs Hailsham-Brown goes and talks to her,' the Inspector told him. 'But she's not to talk to those three men. We'll have no comparing of stories, and no prompting. I hope you locked the door from the library to the hall?'

'Yes, sir,' the Constable assured him. 'I've got the key here.'

'I don't know what to make of them at all,' the Inspector confessed to his colleague. 'They're all highly respectable people. Hailsham-Brown's a Foreign Office diplomat, Hugo Birch is a JP whom we know, and Hailsham-Brown's other two guests seem decent upper-class types — well, you know what I mean . . . But there's something funny going on. None of them are being straightforward with us — and that includes Mrs Hailsham-Brown. They're hiding something, and I'm determined to find out what it is, whether it's got anything to do with this murder or not.'

He stretched his arms above his head as though seeking inspiration from on high, and then addressed the Constable again. 'Well, we'd better get on with it,' he said. 'Let's take them one at a time.'

As the Constable got to his feet, the Inspector changed his mind. 'No. Just a moment. First I'll have a word with that butler chap,' he decided.

'Elgin?'

'Yes, Elgin. Call him in. I've got an idea he knows something.'

'Certainly, sir,' the Constable replied.

Leaving the room, he found Elgin hovering near the sitting-room door. The butler made a tentative pretence of heading for the stairs, but stopped when the Constable called him and came into the room rather nervously.

The Constable closed the hall door and resumed his place for note-taking, while the Inspector indicated the chair near the bridge table.

Elgin sat down, and the Inspector began his interrogation. 'Now, you started off for the

131

pictures this evening,' he reminded the butler, 'but you came back. Why was that?'

'I've told you, sir,' Elgin replied. 'My wife wasn't feeling well.'

The Inspector regarded him steadily. 'It was you who let Mr Costello into the house when he called here this evening, was it not?' he asked.

'Yes, sir.'

The Inspector took a few paces away from Elgin, and then turned back suddenly. 'Why didn't you tell us at once that it was Mr Costello's car outside?' he asked.

'I didn't know whose car it was, sir. Mr Costello didn't drive up to the front door. I didn't even know he'd come in a car.'

'Wasn't that rather peculiar? Leaving his car around by the stables?' the Inspector suggested.

'Well, yes, sir, I suppose it was,' the butler replied. 'But I expect he had his reasons.'

'Just what do you mean by that?' the Inspector asked quickly.

'Nothing, sir,' Elgin answered. He sounded almost smug. 'Nothing at all.'

'Had you ever seen Mr Costello before?' The Inspector's voice was sharp as he asked this.

'Never, sir,' Elgin assured him.

The Inspector adopted a meaning tone to

enquire, 'It wasn't because of Mr Costello that you came back this evening?'

'I've told you, sir,' said Elgin. 'My wife — '

'I don't want to hear any more about your wife,' the Inspector interrupted. Moving away from Elgin, he continued, 'How long have you been with Mrs Hailsham-Brown?'

'Six weeks, sir,' was the reply.

The Inspector turned back to face Elgin. 'And before that?'

'I'd — I'd been having a little rest,' the butler replied uneasily.

'A rest?' the Inspector echoed, in a tone of suspicion. He paused and then added, 'You do realize that, in a case like this, your references will have to be looked into very carefully.'

Elgin began to get to his feet. 'Will that be all — ' he started to say, and then stopped and resumed his seat. 'I — I wouldn't wish to deceive you, sir,' he continued. 'It wasn't anything really wrong. What I mean is — the original reference having got torn — I couldn't quite remember the wording — '

'So you wrote your own references,' the Inspector interrupted. 'That's what it comes to, doesn't it?'

'I didn't mean any harm,' Elgin protested. 'I've got my living to earn — '

The Inspector interrupted him again. 'At

the moment, I'm not interested in fake references,' he told the butler. 'I want to know what happened here tonight, and what you know about Mr Costello.'

'I'd never set eyes on him before,' Elgin insisted. Looking around at the hall door, he continued, 'But I've got a good idea of why he came here.'

'Oh, and what is that?' the Inspector wanted to know.

'Blackmail,' Elgin told him. 'He had something on her.'

'By 'her',' said the Inspector, 'I assume you mean Mrs Hailsham-Brown.'

'Yes,' Elgin continued eagerly. 'I came in to ask if there was anything more she wanted, and I heard them talking.'

'What did you hear exactly?'

'I heard her say 'But that's blackmail. I won't submit to it'.' Elgin adopted a highly dramatic tone as he quoted Clarissa's words.

'Hm!' the Inspector responded a little doubtfully. 'Anything more?'

'No,' Elgin admitted. 'They stopped when I came in, and when I went out they dropped their voices.'

'I see,' the Inspector commented. He looked intently at the butler, waiting for him to speak again.

Elgin got up from his chair. His voice was

almost a whine as he pleaded, 'You won't be hard on me, sir, will you? I've had a lot of trouble one way and another.'

The Inspector regarded him for a moment longer, and then said dismissively, 'Oh, that will do. Get out.'

'Yes, sir. Thank you, sir,' Elgin responded quickly as he made a hasty exit into the hall.

The Inspector watched him go, and then turned to the Constable. 'Blackmail, eh?' he murmured, exchanging glances with his colleague.

'And Mrs Hailsham-Brown such a nice seeming lady,' Constable Jones observed with a somewhat prim look.

'Yes, well one never can tell,' the Inspector observed. He paused, and then ordered curtly, 'I'll see Mr Birch now.' The Constable went to the library door. 'Mr Birch, please.'

Hugo came through the library door, looking dogged and rather defiant. The Constable closed the door behind him and took a seat at the table, while the Inspector greeted Hugo pleasantly. 'Come in, Mr Birch,' he invited. 'Sit down here, please.'

Hugo sat, and the Inspector continued, 'This is a very unpleasant business, I'm afraid, sir. What have you to tell us about it?'

Slapping his spectacle case on the table, Hugo replied defiantly, 'Absolutely nothing.'

'Nothing?' queried the Inspector, sounding surprised.

'What do you expect me to say?' Hugo expostulated. 'The blinking woman snaps open the blinking cupboard, and out falls a blinking corpse.' He gave a snort of impatience. 'Took my breath away,' he declared. 'I've not got over it yet.' He glared at the Inspector. 'It's no good asking me anything,' he said firmly, 'because I don't know anything about it.'

The Inspector regarded Hugo steadily for a moment before asking, 'That's your statement, is it? Just that you know nothing at all about it?'

'I'm telling you,' Hugo repeated. 'I didn't kill the fellow.' Again he glared defiantly. 'I didn't even know him.'

'You didn't know him,' the Inspector repeated. 'Very well. I'm not suggesting that you did know him. I'm certainly not suggesting that you murdered him. But I can't believe that you 'know nothing', as you put it. So let's collaborate to find out what you do know. To begin with, you'd heard of him, hadn't you?'

'Yes,' snapped Hugo, 'and I'd heard he was a nasty bit of goods.'

'In what way?' the Inspector asked calmly.

'Oh, I don't know,' Hugo blustered. 'He was the sort of fellow that women liked and men had no use for. That sort of thing.'

The Inspector paused before asking carefully, 'You've no idea why he should come back to this house a second time this evening?'

'Not a clue,' replied Hugo dismissively.

The Inspector took a few steps around the room, then turned abruptly to face Hugo. 'Was there anything between him and the present Mrs Hailsham-Brown, do you think?' he asked.

Hugo looked shocked. 'Clarissa? Good Lord, no! Nice girl, Clarissa. Got a lot of sense. She wouldn't look twice at a fellow like that.'

The Inspector paused again, and then said, finally, 'So you can't help us.'

'Sorry. But there it is,' replied Hugo with an attempt at nonchalance.

Making one last effort to extract at least a crumb of information from Hugo, the Inspector asked, 'Had you really no idea that the body was in that recess?'

'Of course not,' replied Hugo, now sounding offended.

'Thank you, sir,' said the Inspector, turning away from him.

'What?' queried Hugo vaguely.

'That's all, thank you, sir,' the Inspector repeated. He went to the desk and picked up a red book that lay on it.

Hugo rose, picked up his spectacle case, and was about to go across to the library door when the Constable got up and barred his way. Hugo then turned towards the French windows, but the Constable said, 'This way, Mr Birch, please,' and opened the hall door. Giving up, Hugo went out and the policeman closed the door behind him.

The Inspector carried his huge red book over to the bridge table, and sat consulting it, as Constable Jones commented satirically, 'Mr Birch was a mine of information, wasn't he? Mind you, it's not very nice for a JP to be mixed up in a murder.'

The Inspector began to read aloud. ''Delahaye, Sir Rowland Edward Mark, KCB, MVO — ''

'What have you got there?' the Constable asked. He peered over the Inspector's shoulder. 'Oh, *Who's Who.*'

The Inspector went on reading. ''Educated Eton — Trinity College — ' Um! 'Attached Foreign Office — second Secretary — Madrid — Plenipotentiary'.'

'Ooh!' the Constable exclaimed at this last word.

The Inspector gave him an exasperated look, and continued, ''Constantinople, Foreign Office — special commission rendered — Clubs — Boodles — Whites'.'

'Do you want him next, sir?' the Constable asked.

The Inspector thought for a moment. 'No,' he decided. 'He's the most interesting of the lot, so I'll leave him till the last. Let's have young Warrender in now.'

15

Constable Jones, standing at the library door, called, 'Mr Warrender, please.'

Jeremy came in, attempting rather unsuccessfully to look completely at his ease. The Constable closed the door and resumed his seat at the table, while the Inspector half rose and pulled out a chair from the bridge table for Jeremy.

'Sit down,' he ordered somewhat brusquely as he resumed his seat. Jeremy sat, and the Inspector asked formally, 'Your name?'

'Jeremy Warrender.'

'Address?'

'Three hundred and forty, Broad Street, and thirty-four Grosvenor Square,' Jeremy told him, trying to sound nonchalant. He glanced across at the Constable who was writing all this down, and added, 'Country address, Hepplestone, Wiltshire.'

'That sounds as though you're a gentleman of independent means,' the Inspector commented.

'I'm afraid not,' Jeremy admitted, with a smile. 'I'm private secretary to Sir Kenneth Thomson, the Chairman of Saxon-Arabian Oil. Those are his addresses.'

The Inspector nodded. 'I see. How long have you been with him?'

'About a year. Before that, I was personal assistant to Mr Scott Agius for four years.'

'Ah, yes,' said the Inspector. 'He's that wealthy businessman in the City, isn't he?' He thought for a moment before going on to ask, 'Did you know this man, Oliver Costello?'

'No, I'd never heard of him till tonight,' Jeremy told him.

'And you didn't see him when he came to the house earlier this evening?' the Inspector continued.

'No,' Jeremy replied. 'I'd gone over to the golf club with the others. We were dining there, you see. It was the servants' night out, and Mr Birch had asked us to dine with him at the club.'

The Inspector nodded his head. After a pause, he asked, 'Was Mrs Hailsham-Brown invited, too?'

'No, she wasn't,' said Jeremy.

The Inspector raised his eyebrows, and Jeremy hurried on. 'That is,' he explained, 'she could have come if she'd liked.'

'Do you mean,' the Inspector asked him, 'that she was asked, then? And she refused?'

'No, no,' Jeremy replied hurriedly, sounding as though he was getting rattled. 'What I mean is — well, Hailsham-Brown is usually quite tired by the time he gets down here, and Clarissa said they'd just have a scratch meal here, as usual.'

The Inspector looked confused. 'Let me get this clear,' he said rather snappily. 'Mrs Hailsham-Brown expected her husband to dine here? She didn't expect him to go out again as soon as he came in?'

Jeremy was now quite definitely flustered. 'I — er — well — er — really, I don't know,' he stammered. 'No — Now that you mention it, I believe she did say he was going to be out this evening.'

The Inspector rose and took a few paces away from Jeremy. 'It seems odd, then,' he observed, 'that Mrs Hailsham-Brown should not have come out to the club with the three of you, instead of remaining here to dine all by herself.'

Jeremy turned on his chair to face the Inspector. 'Well — er — well — ' he began, and then, gaining confidence, continued quickly, 'I mean, it was the kid — Pippa, you know. Clarissa wouldn't have liked to go out and leave the kid all by herself in the house.'

'Or perhaps,' the Inspector suggested, speaking with heavy significance, 'perhaps she was making plans to receive a visitor of her own?'

Jeremy rose to his feet. 'I say, that's a rotten

thing to suggest,' he exclaimed hotly. 'And it isn't true. I'm sure she never planned anything of the kind.'

'Yet Oliver Costello came here to meet someone,' the Inspector pointed out. 'The two servants had the night off. Miss Peake has her own cottage. There was really no one he could have come to the house to meet except Mrs Hailsham-Brown.'

'All I can say is — ' Jeremy began. Then, turning away, he added limply, 'Well, you'd better ask her.'

'I have asked her,' the Inspector informed him.

'What did she say?' asked Jeremy, turning back to face the police officer.

'Just what you say,' the Inspector replied suavely.

Jeremy sat down again at the bridge table. 'There you are, then,' he observed.

The Inspector took a few steps around the room, his eyes on the floor as though deep in thought. Then he turned back to face Jeremy. 'Now tell me,' he queried, 'just how you all happened to come back here from the club. Was that your original plan?'

'Yes,' Jeremy replied, but then quickly changed his answer. 'I mean, no.'

'Which do you mean, sir?' the Inspector queried smoothly.

Jeremy took a deep breath. 'Well,' he began, 'it was like this. We all went over to the club. Sir Rowland and old Hugo went straight into the dining-room and I came in a bit later. It's all a cold buffet, you know. I'd been knocking balls about until it got dark, and then — well, somebody said 'Bridge, anyone?', and I said, 'Well, why don't we go back to the Hailsham-Browns' where it's more cosy, and play there?' So we did.'

'I see,' observed the Inspector. 'So it was your idea?'

Jeremy shrugged his shoulders. 'I really don't remember who suggested it first,' he admitted. 'It may have been Hugo Birch, I think.'

'And you arrived back here — when?'

Jeremy thought for a moment, and then shook his head. 'I can't say exactly,' he murmured. 'We probably left the club house just a bit before eight.'

'And it's — what?' the Inspector wondered. 'Five minutes' walk?'

'Yes, just about that. The golf course adjoins this garden,' Jeremy answered, glancing out of the window.

The Inspector went across to the bridge table, and looked down at its surface. 'And then you played bridge?'

'Yes,' Jeremy confirmed.

The Inspector nodded his head slowly. 'That must have been about twenty minutes before my arrival here,' he calculated. He began to walk slowly around the table. 'Surely you didn't have time to complete two rubbers and start — ' he held up Clarissa's marker so that Jeremy could see it — 'a third?'

'What?' Jeremy looked confused for a moment, but then said quickly, 'Oh, no. No. That first rubber must have been yesterday's score.'

Indicating the other markers, the Inspector remarked thoughtfully, 'Only one person seems to have scored.'

'Yes,' Jeremy agreed. 'I'm afraid we're all a bit lazy about scoring. We left it to Clarissa.'

The Inspector walked across to the sofa. 'Did you know about the passage-way between this room and the library?' he asked.

'You mean the place where the body was found?'

'That's what I mean.'

'No. No, I'd no idea,' Jeremy asserted. 'Wonderful bit of camouflage, isn't it? You'd never guess it was there.'

The Inspector sat on an arm of the sofa, leaning back and dislodging a cushion. He noticed the gloves that had been lying under the cushion. His face wore a serious expression as he said quietly, 'Consequently,

Mr Warrender, you couldn't know there was a body in that passage-way. Could you?'

Jeremy turned away. 'You could have knocked me over with a feather, as the saying goes,' he replied. 'Absolute blood and thunder melodrama. Couldn't believe my eyes.'

While Jeremy was speaking, the Inspector had been sorting out the gloves on the sofa. He now held up one pair of them, rather in the manner of a conjuror. 'By the way, are these your gloves, Mr Warrender?' he asked, trying to sound off-handed.

Jeremy turned back to him. 'No. I mean, yes,' he replied confusedly.

'Again, which do you mean, sir?'

'Yes, they are mine, I think.'

'Were you wearing them when you came back here from the golf club?'

'Yes,' Jeremy recalled. 'I remember now. Yes, I was wearing them. There's a bit of a nip in the air this evening.'

The Inspector got up from the arm of the sofa, and approached Jeremy. 'I think you're mistaken, sir.' Indicating the initials in the gloves, he pointed out, 'These have Mr Hailsham-Brown's initials inside them.'

Returning his gaze calmly, Jeremy replied, 'Oh, that's funny. I've got a pair just the same.'

The Inspector returned to the sofa, sat on the arm again and, leaning over, produced the second pair of gloves. 'Perhaps these are yours?' he suggested.

Jeremy laughed. 'You don't catch me a second time,' he replied. 'After all, one pair of gloves looks exactly like another.'

The Inspector produced the third pair of gloves. 'Three pairs of gloves,' he murmured, examining them. 'All with Hailsham-Brown's initials inside. Curious.'

'Well, it is his house, after all,' Jeremy pointed out. 'Why shouldn't he have three pairs of gloves lying about?'

'The only interesting thing,' the Inspector replied, 'is that you thought one of them might have been yours. And I think that your gloves are just sticking out of your pocket, now.'

Jeremy put his hand in his right-hand pocket. 'No, the other one,' the Inspector told him.

Removing the gloves from his left-hand pocket, Jeremy exclaimed, 'Oh yes. Yes, so they are.'

'They're not really very like these. Are they?' the Inspector asked, pointedly.

'Actually, these are my golfing gloves,' Jeremy replied with a smile.

'Thank you, Mr Warrender,' the Inspector

147

said abruptly and dismissively, patting the cushion back into place on the sofa. 'That will be all for now.'

Jeremy rose, looking upset. 'Look here,' he exclaimed, 'you don't think — ' He paused.

'I don't think what, sir?' asked the Inspector.

'Nothing,' Jeremy replied uncertainly. He paused, and then made for the library door, only to be intercepted by the Constable. Turning back to the Inspector, Jeremy pointed mutely and enquiringly at the hall door. The Inspector nodded, and Jeremy made his way out of the room, closing the hall door behind him.

Leaving the gloves on the sofa, the Inspector went across to the bridge table, sat, and consulted *Who's Who* again. 'Here we are,' he murmured, and began to read aloud, ' "Thomson, Sir Kenneth. Chairman of Saxon-Arabian Oil Company, Gulf Petroleum Company.' Hmm! Impressive. 'Recreations: Philately, golf, fishing. Address, three hundred and forty Broad Street, thirty-four Grosvenor Square'.'

While the Inspector was reading, Constable Jones went across to the table by the sofa and began to sharpen his pencil into the ashtray. Stooping to pick up some shavings from the floor, he saw a playing-card lying there and brought it to the bridge table, throwing it down in front of his superior.

'What have you got there?' the Inspector asked.

'Just a card, sir. Found it over there, under the sofa.'

The Inspector picked up the card. 'The ace of spades,' he noted. 'A very interesting card. Here, wait a minute.' He turned the card over. 'Red. It's the same pack.' He picked up the red pack of cards from the table, and spread them out.

The Constable helped him sort through the cards. 'Well, well, no ace of spades,' the Inspector exclaimed. He rose from his chair. 'Now, that's very remarkable, don't you think, Jones?' he asked, putting the card in his pocket and going across to the sofa. 'They managed to play bridge without missing the ace of spades.'

'Very remarkable indeed, sir,' Constable Jones agreed, as he tidied the cards on the table.

The Inspector collected the three pairs of gloves from the sofa. 'Now I think we'll have Sir Rowland Delahaye,' he instructed the Constable, as he took the gloves to the bridge table and spread them out in pairs.

16

The Constable opened the library door, calling, 'Sir Rowland Delahaye.'

As Sir Rowland paused in the doorway, the Inspector called, 'Do come in, sir, and sit down here, please.'

Sir Rowland approached the bridge table, paused for a moment as he noticed the gloves spread out on it, and then sat.

'You are Sir Rowland Delahaye?' the Inspector asked him formally. Receiving a grave, affirmative nod, he next asked, 'What is your address?'

'Long Paddock, Littlewich Green, Lincolnshire,' Sir Rowland replied. Tapping a finger on the copy of *Who's Who*, he added, 'Couldn't you find it, Inspector?'

The Inspector chose to ignore this. 'Now, if you please,' he said, 'I'd like your account of the evening, after you left here shortly before seven.'

Sir Rowland had obviously already given some thought to this. 'It had been raining all day,' he began smoothly, 'and then it suddenly cleared up. We had already arranged to go to the golf club for dinner, as it is the servants' night out. So we did that.' He glanced across at the Constable, as though to make sure he was keeping up, then continued, 'As we were finishing dinner, Mrs Hailsham-Brown rang up and suggested that, as her husband had unexpectedly had to go out, we three should return here and make up a four for bridge. We did so. About twenty minutes after we'd started playing, you arrived, Inspector. The rest — you know.'

The Inspector looked thoughtful. 'That's not quite Mr Warrender's account of the matter,' he observed.

'Indeed?' said Sir Rowland. 'And how did he put it?'

'He said that the suggestion to come back here and play bridge came from one of you. But he thought it was probably Mr Birch.'

'Ah,' replied Sir Rowland easily, 'but you see Warrender came into the dining-room at the club rather late. He did not realize that Mrs Hailsham-Brown had rung up.'

Sir Rowland and the Inspector looked at each other, as though trying to stare each other out. Then Sir Rowland continued, 'You must know better than I do, Inspector, how very rarely two people's accounts of the same thing agree. In fact, if the three of us were to agree exactly, I should regard it as suspicious. Very suspicious indeed.'

The Inspector chose not to comment on this observation. Drawing a chair up close to Sir Rowland, he sat down. 'I'd like to discuss the case with you, sir, if I may,' he suggested.

'How very agreeable of you, Inspector,' Sir Rowland replied.

After looking thoughtfully at the table-top for a few seconds, the Inspector began the discussion. 'The dead man, Mr Oliver Costello, came to this house with some particular object in view.' He paused. 'Do you agree that that is what must have happened, sir?'

'My understanding is that he came to return to Henry Hailsham-Brown certain objects which Mrs Miranda Hailsham-Brown, as she then was, had taken away in error,' Sir Rowland replied.

'That may have been his excuse, sir,' the Inspector pointed out, 'though I'm not even sure of that. But I'm certain it wasn't the real reason that brought him here.'

Sir Rowland shrugged his shoulders. 'You may be right,' he observed. 'I can't say.'

The Inspector pressed on. 'He came, perhaps, to see a particular person. It may have been you, it may have been Mr Warrender, or it may have been Mr Birch.'

'If he had wanted to see Mr Birch, who lives locally,' Sir Rowland pointed out, 'he

152

would have gone to his house. He wouldn't have come here.'

'That is probably so,' the Inspector agreed. 'Therefore that leaves us with the choice of four people. You, Mr Warrender, Mr Hailsham-Brown and Mrs Hailsham-Brown.' He paused and gave Sir Rowland a searching glance before asking, 'Now, sir, how well did you know Oliver Costello?'

'Hardly at all. I've met him once or twice, that's all.'

'Where did you meet him?' asked the Inspector.

Sir Rowland reflected. 'Twice at the Hailsham-Browns' in London, over a year ago, and once in a restaurant, I believe.'

'But you had no reason for wishing to murder him?'

'Is that an accusation, Inspector?' Sir Rowland asked with a smile.

The Inspector shook his head. 'No, Sir Rowland,' he replied. 'I should call it more an elimination. I don't think you have any motive for doing away with Oliver Costello. So that leaves just three people.'

'This is beginning to sound like a variant of 'Ten Little Indians',' Sir Rowland observed with a smile.

The Inspector smiled back. 'We'll take Mr Warrender next,' he proposed. 'Now, how

153

well do you know him?'

'I met him here for the first time two days ago,' Sir Rowland replied. 'He appears to be an agreeable young man, well bred, and well educated. He's a friend of Clarissa's. I know nothing about him, but I should say he's an unlikely murderer.'

'So much for Mr Warrender,' the Inspector noted. 'That brings me to my next question.'

Anticipating him, Sir Rowland nodded. 'How well do I know Henry Hailsham-Brown, and how well do I know Mrs Hailsham-Brown? That's what you want to know, isn't it?' he asked. 'Actually, I know Henry Hailsham-Brown very well indeed. He is an old friend. As for Clarissa, I know all there is to know about her. She is my ward, and inexpressibly dear to me.'

'Yes, sir,' said the Inspector. 'I think that answer makes certain things very clear.'

'Does it, indeed?'

The Inspector rose and took a few paces about the room before turning back to face Sir Rowland. 'Why did you three change your plans this evening?' he asked. 'Why did you come back here and pretend to play bridge?'

'Pretend?' Sir Rowland exclaimed sharply.

The Inspector took the playing card from his pocket. 'This card,' he said, 'was found on

154

the other side of the room under the sofa. I can hardly believe that you would have played two rubbers of bridge and started a third with a pack of fifty-one cards, and the ace of spades missing.'

Sir Rowland took the card from the Inspector, looked at the back of it, and then returned it. 'Yes,' he admitted. 'Perhaps that is a little difficult to believe.'

The Inspector cast his eyes despairingly upwards before adding, 'I also think that three pairs of Mr Hailsham-Brown's gloves need a certain amount of explanation.'

After a moment's pause, Sir Rowland replied, 'I'm afraid, Inspector, you won't get any explanation from me.'

'No, sir,' the Inspector agreed. 'I take it that you are out to do your best for a certain lady. But it's not a bit of good, sir. The truth will out.'

'I wonder if it will,' was Sir Rowland's only response to this observation.

The Inspector went across to the panel. 'Mrs Hailsham-Brown knew that Costello's body was in the recess,' he insisted. 'Whether she dragged it there herself, or whether you helped her, I don't know. But I'm convinced that she knew.' He came back to face Sir Rowland. 'I suggest,' he continued, 'that Oliver Costello came here to see Mrs

Hailsham-Brown and to obtain money from her by threats.'

'Threats?' Sir Rowland asked. 'Threats of what?'

'That will all come out in due course, I have no doubt,' the Inspector assured him. 'Mrs Hailsham-Brown is young and attractive. This Mr Costello was a great man for the ladies, they say. Now, Mrs Hailsham-Brown is newly married and — '

'Stop!' Sir Rowland interrupted peremptorily. 'I must put you right on certain matters. You can confirm what I tell you easily enough. Henry Hailsham-Brown's first marriage was unfortunate. His wife, Miranda, was a beautiful woman, but unbalanced and neurotic. Her health and disposition had degenerated to such an alarming state that her little daughter had to be removed to a nursing home.'

He paused in reflection. Then, 'Yes, a really shocking state of affairs,' he continued. 'It seemed that Miranda had become a drug addict. How she obtained these drugs was not found out, but it was a very fair guess that she had been supplied with them by this man, Oliver Costello. She was infatuated with him, and finally ran away with him.'

After another pause and a glance across at the Constable, to see if he was keeping up, Sir

156

Rowland resumed his story. 'Henry Hailsham-Brown, who is old-fashioned in his views, allowed Miranda to divorce him,' he explained. 'Henry has now found happiness and peace in his marriage with Clarissa, and I can assure you, Inspector, that there are no guilty secrets in Clarissa's life. There is nothing, I can swear, with which Costello could possibly threaten her.'

The Inspector said nothing, but merely looked thoughtful.

Sir Rowland stood up, tucked his chair under the table, and walked over to the sofa. Then, turning to address the police officer again, he suggested, 'Don't you think, Inspector, that you're on the wrong track altogether? Why should you be so certain that it was a person Costello came here to see? Why couldn't it have been a place?'

The Inspector now looked perplexed. 'What do you mean, sir?' he asked.

'When you were talking to us about the late Mr Sellon,' Sir Rowland reminded him, 'you mentioned that the Narcotics Squad took an interest in him. Isn't there a possible link there? Drugs — Sellon — Sellon's house?'

He paused but, receiving no reaction from the Inspector, continued, 'Costello has been here once before, I understand, ostensibly to look at Sellon's antiques. Supposing Oliver

Costello wanted something in this house. In that desk, perhaps.'

The Inspector glanced at the desk, and Sir Rowland expanded on his theory. 'There is the curious incident of a man who came here and offered an exorbitant price for that desk. Supposing it was that desk that Oliver Costello wanted to examine — wanted to search, if you like. Supposing that he was followed here by someone. And that that someone struck him down, there by the desk.'

The Inspector did not seem impressed. 'There's a good deal of supposition — ' he began, only to be interrupted by Sir Rowland who insisted, 'It's a very reasonable hypothesis.'

'The hypothesis being,' the Inspector queried, 'that this somebody put the body in the recess?'

'Exactly.'

'That would have to be somebody who knew about the recess,' the Inspector observed.

'It could be someone who knew the house in Sellon's time,' Sir Rowland pointed out.

'Yes, that's all very well, sir,' the Inspector replied impatiently, 'but it still doesn't explain one thing — '

'What is that?' asked Sir Rowland.

The Inspector looked at him steadily. 'Mrs

Hailsham-Brown knew the body was in that recess. She tried to prevent us looking there.'

Sir Rowland opened his mouth to speak, but the Inspector held up a hand and continued, 'It's no good trying to convince me otherwise. She knew.'

For a few moments, a tense silence prevailed. Then Sir Rowland said, 'Inspector, will you allow me to speak to my ward?'

'Only in my presence, sir,' was the prompt reply.

'That will do.'

The Inspector nodded. 'Jones!' The Constable, understanding what was required, left the room.

'We are very much in your hands, Inspector,' Sir Rowland told the police officer. 'I will ask you to make what allowances you can.'

'My one concern is to get at the truth, sir, and to find out who killed Oliver Costello,' the Inspector replied.

17

The Constable came back into the room, holding the door open for Clarissa.

'Come in here, please, Mrs Hailsham-Brown,' the Inspector called. As Clarissa entered, Sir Rowland went over to her. He spoke very solemnly. 'Clarissa, my dear,' he said. 'Will you do what I ask you? I want you to tell the Inspector the truth.'

'The truth?' Clarissa echoed, sounding very doubtful.

'The truth,' Sir Rowland repeated with emphasis. 'It's the only thing to do. I mean it. Seriously.' He looked at her steadily and indeed seriously for a moment, and then left the room. The Constable closed the door after him and resumed his seat for note-taking.

'Do sit down, Mrs Hailsham-Brown,' the Inspector invited her, this time indicating the sofa.

Clarissa smiled at him, but the look he returned was a stern one. She moved slowly to the sofa, sat, and waited for a moment before speaking. Then, 'I'm sorry,' she told him. 'I'm terribly sorry I told you all those lies. I didn't mean to.' She did indeed sound rueful as she continued, 'One gets into things, if you know what I mean?'

'I can't say that I do know,' the Inspector replied coldly. 'Now, please just give me the facts.'

'Well, it's really all quite simple,' she explained, ticking off the facts on her fingers as she spoke. 'First, Oliver Costello left. Then, Henry came home. Then, I saw him off again in the car. Then, I came in here with the sandwiches.'

'Sandwiches?' the Inspector queried.

'Yes. You see, my husband is bringing home a very important delegate from abroad.'

The Inspector looked interested. 'Oh, who is this deleegate?'

'A Mr Jones,' Clarissa told him.

'I beg your pardon?' said the Inspector, with a look at Constable Jones.

'Mr Jones. That's not his real name, but that's what we have to call him. It's all very hush-hush.' Clarissa went on speaking. 'They were going to have the sandwiches while they talked, and I was going to have mousse in the schoolroom.'

The Inspector was looking perplexed. 'Mousse in the — yes, I see,' he murmured, sounding as though he did not see at all.

'I put the sandwiches down there,' Clarissa told him, pointing to the stool, 'and then I began tidying up, and I went to put a book back on the bookshelf and — then — and then I practically fell over it.'

'You fell over the body?' the Inspector asked.

'Yes. It was here, behind the sofa. And I looked to see if it — if he was dead, and he was. It was Oliver Costello, and I didn't know what to do. In the end, I rang up the golf club, and I asked Sir Rowland, Mr Birch and Jeremy Warrender to come back right away.'

Leaning over the sofa, the Inspector asked coldly, 'It didn't occur to you to ring up the police?'

'Well, it occurred to me, yes,' Clarissa answered, 'but then — well — ' She smiled at him again. 'Well, I didn't.'

'You didn't,' the Inspector murmured to himself. He walked away, looked at the Constable, lifted his hands despairingly, and then turned back to face Clarissa. 'Why didn't you ring the police?' he asked her.

Clarissa was prepared for this. 'Well, I didn't think it would be nice for my husband,' she replied. 'I don't know whether you know many people in the Foreign Office, Inspector, but they're frightfully unassuming. They like everything very quiet, not noticeable. You must admit that murders are rather noticeable.'

'Quite so,' was all that the Inspector could think of in response to this.

'I'm so glad you understand,' Clarissa told him warmly and almost gushingly. She went on with her story, but her delivery became more and more unconvincing as she began to feel that she was not making headway. 'I mean,' she said, 'he was quite dead, because I felt his pulse, so we couldn't do anything for him.'

The Inspector walked about, without replying. Following him with her eyes, Clarissa continued, 'What I mean is, he might just as well be dead in Marsden Wood as in our drawing-room.'

The Inspector turned sharply to face her. 'Marsden Wood?' he asked abruptly. 'How does Marsden Wood come into it?'

'That's where I was thinking of putting him,' Clarissa replied.

The Inspector put a hand to the back of his head, and looked at the floor as though seeking inspiration there. Then, shaking his head to clear it, he said firmly, 'Mrs Hailsham-Brown, have you never heard that a dead body, if there's any suggestion of foul play, should never be moved?'

'Of course I know that,' Clarissa retorted. 'It says so in all the detective stories. But, you see, this is real life.'

The Inspector lifted his hands in despair.

'I mean,' she continued, 'real life's quite different.'

The Inspector looked at Clarissa in incredulous silence for a moment, before asking her, 'Do you realize the seriousness of what you're saying?'

'Of course I do,' she replied, 'and I'm telling you the truth. So, you see, in the end, I rang up the club and they all came back here.'

'And you persuaded them to hide the body in that recess.'

'No,' Clarissa corrected him. 'That came later. My plan, as I told you, was that they should take Oliver's body away in his car and leave the car in Marsden Wood.'

'And they agreed?' The Inspector's tone was distinctly unbelieving.

'Yes, they agreed,' said Clarissa, smiling at him.

'Frankly, Mrs Hailsham-Brown,' the Inspector told her brusquely, 'I don't believe a word of it. I don't believe that three responsible men would agree to obstruct the course of justice in such a manner for such a paltry cause.'

Clarissa rose to her feet. Walking away from the Inspector, she said more to herself than to him, 'I knew you wouldn't believe me if I told you the truth.' She turned to face him. 'What *do* you believe, then?' she asked him.

Watching Clarissa closely as he spoke, the Inspector replied, 'I can see only one reason why those three men should agree to lie.'

'Oh? What do you mean? What other reason would they have?'

'They would agree to lie,' the Inspector continued, 'if they believed, or, even more so, if they actually knew — that you had killed him.'

Clarissa stared at him. 'But I had no *reason* for killing him,' she protested. 'Absolutely no reason.' She flung away from him. 'Oh, I knew you'd react like this,' she exclaimed. 'That's why — '

She broke off suddenly, and the Inspector turned to her. 'That's why what?' he asked abruptly.

Clarissa stood thinking. Some moments passed, and then her manner appeared to change. She began to speak more convincingly. 'All right, then,' she announced, with the air of one who is making a clean breast of things. 'I'll tell you why.'

'I think that would be wiser,' the Inspector said.

'Yes,' she agreed, turning to face him squarely. 'I suppose I'd better tell you the *truth*.' She emphasized the word.

The Inspector smiled. 'I can assure you,' he advised her, 'that telling the police a pack of lies will do you very little good, Mrs Hailsham-Brown. You'd better tell me the real story. And from the beginning.'

'I will,' Clarissa promised. She sat down in a chair by the bridge table. 'Oh dear,' she sighed, 'I thought I was being so clever.'

'It's much better not to try to be clever,' the Inspector told her. He seated himself facing Clarissa. 'Now then,' he asked, 'what really did happen this evening?'

18

Clarissa was silent for a few moments. Then, looking the Inspector steadily in the eye, she began to speak. 'It all started as I've already explained to you. I said good-bye to Oliver Costello, and he'd gone off with Miss Peake. I had no idea he would come back again, and I still can't understand why he did.'

She paused, and seemed to be trying to recall what had happened next. 'Oh, yes,' she continued. 'Then my husband came home, explaining that he would have to go out again immediately. He went off in the car, and it was just after I had shut the front door, and made sure that it was latched and bolted, that I suddenly began to feel nervous.'

'Nervous?' asked the Inspector, looking puzzled. 'Why?'

'Well, I'm not usually nervous,' she told him, speaking with great feeling, 'but it occurred to me that I'd never been alone in the house at night.'

She paused. 'Yes, go on,' the Inspector encouraged her.

'I told myself not to be so silly. I said to myself, 'You've got the phone, haven't you?

You can always ring for help.' I said to myself, 'Burglars don't come at this time of the evening. They come in the middle of the night.' But I still kept thinking I heard a door shutting somewhere, or footsteps up in my bedroom. So I thought I'd better do something.'

She paused again, and again the Inspector prompted her. 'Yes?'

'I went into the kitchen,' Clarissa said, 'and made the sandwiches for Henry and Mr Jones to have when they got back. I got them all ready on a plate, with a napkin around them to keep them soft, and I was just coming across the hall to put them in here, when — ' she paused dramatically — 'I really heard something.'

'Where?' the Inspector asked.

'In this room,' she told him. 'I knew that, this time, I wasn't imagining it. I heard drawers being pulled open and shut, and then I suddenly remembered that the French windows in here weren't locked. We never do lock them. Somebody had come in that way.'

Again she paused. 'Go on, Mrs Hailsham-Brown,' said the Inspector impassively.

Clarissa made a gesture of helplessness. 'I didn't know what to do. I was petrified. Then I thought, 'What if I'm just being a fool? What if it's Henry come back for something

— or even Sir Rowland or one of the others? A nice fool you'll look if you go upstairs and ring the police on the extension.' So then I thought of a plan.'

She paused once more, and the Inspector's 'Yes?' this time sounded a trifle impatient.

'I went to the hall stand,' Clarissa said slowly, 'and I took the heaviest stick I could find. Then I went into the library. I didn't turn the light on. I felt my way across the room to that recess. I opened it very gently and slipped inside. I thought I could ease the door into here and see who it was.' She pointed to the panel. 'Unless anyone knew about it, you'd never dream there was a door just there.'

'No,' the Inspector agreed, 'you certainly wouldn't.'

Clarissa seemed now to be almost enjoying her narrative. 'I eased the catch open,' she continued, 'and then my fingers slipped, and the door swung right open and hit against a chair. A man who was standing by the desk straightened up. I saw something bright and shining in his hand. I thought it was a revolver. I was terrified. I thought he was going to shoot me. I hit out at him with the stick with all my might, and he fell.'

She collapsed and leant on the table with her face in her hands. 'Could I — could I have a little brandy, please?' she asked the Inspector.

'Yes, of course.' The Inspector got to his feet. 'Jones!' he called. The Constable poured some brandy into a glass and handed it to the Inspector. Clarissa had lifted her face, but quickly covered it with her hands again and held out her hand as the Inspector brought her the brandy. She drank, coughed, and returned the glass. Constable Jones replaced it on a table and resumed his seat and his note-taking.

The Inspector looked at Clarissa. 'Do you feel able to continue, Mrs Hailsham-Brown?' he asked sympathetically.

'Yes,' Clarissa replied, glancing up at him. 'You're very kind.' She took a breath and continued her story. 'The man just lay there. He didn't move. I switched on the light and I saw then that it was Oliver Costello. He was dead. It was terrible. I — I couldn't understand it.'

She gestured towards the desk. 'I couldn't understand what he was doing there, tampering with the desk. It was all like some ghastly nightmare. I was so frightened that I rang the golf club. I wanted my guardian to be with me. They all came over. I begged them to help me, to take the body away — somewhere.'

The Inspector stared at her intently. 'But why?' he asked.

Clarissa turned away from him. 'Because I was a coward,' she said. 'A miserable coward. I was frightened of the publicity, of having to go to a police court. And it would be so bad for my husband and for his career.'

She turned back to the Inspector. 'If it had really been a burglar, perhaps I could have gone through with it, but being someone we actually knew, someone who is married to Henry's first wife — Oh, I just felt I couldn't go through with it.'

'Perhaps,' the Inspector suggested, 'because the dead man had, a short while before, attempted to blackmail you?'

'Blackmail me? Oh, that's nonsense!' Clarissa replied with complete confidence. 'That's just silly. There's nothing anyone could blackmail me about.'

'Elgin, your butler, overheard a mention of blackmail,' the Inspector told her.

'I don't believe he heard anything of the kind,' replied Clarissa. 'He couldn't. If you ask me, he's making the whole thing up.'

'Come now, Mrs Hailsham-Brown,' the Inspector insisted, 'are you deliberately telling me that the word blackmail was never mentioned? Why would your butler make it up?'

'I swear there was no mention of blackmail,' Clarissa exclaimed, banging the table with her hand. 'I assure you — ' Her hand stopped in mid-air, and she suddenly laughed. 'Oh, how silly. Of course. That was it.'

'You've remembered?' the Inspector asked calmly.

'It was nothing, really,' Clarissa assured him. 'It was just that Oliver was saying something about the rent of furnished houses being absurdly high, and I said we'd been amazingly lucky and were only paying four guineas a week for this. And he said, 'I can hardly believe it, Clarissa. What's your pull? It must be blackmail.' And I laughed and said, 'That's it. Blackmail.''

She laughed now, apparently recalling the exchange. 'Just a silly, joking way of talking. Why, I didn't even remember it.'

'I'm sorry, Mrs Hailsham-Brown,' said the Inspector, 'but I really can't believe that.'

Clarissa looked astonished. 'Can't believe what?'

'That you're only paying four guineas a week for this house, furnished.'

'Honestly! You really are the most unbelieving man I've ever met,' Clarissa told him as she rose and went to the desk. 'You don't seem to believe a single thing I've said to you this evening. Most things I can't prove, but this one I can. And this time I'm going to show you.'

She opened a drawer of the desk and searched through the papers in it. 'Here it is,' she exclaimed. 'No, it isn't. Ah! Here we are.' She took a document from the drawer and showed it to the Inspector. 'Here's the agreement for our tenancy of this house, furnished. It's made out by a firm of solicitors acting for the executors and, look — four guineas per week.'

The Inspector looked jolted. 'Well, I'm blessed! It's extraordinary. Quite extraordinary. I'd have thought it was worth much more than that.'

Clarissa gave him one of her most charming smiles. 'Don't you think, Inspector, that you ought to beg my pardon?' she suggested.

The Inspector injected a certain amount of charm into his voice as he responded. 'I do apologize, Mrs Hailsham-Brown,' he said, 'but it really is extremely odd, you know.'

'Why? What do you mean?' Clarissa asked, as she replaced the document in the drawer.

'Well, it so happens,' the Inspector replied, 'that a lady and a gentleman were down in this area with orders to view this house, and the lady happened to lose a very valuable brooch somewhere in the vicinity. She called in at the police station to give particulars, and she happened to mention this house. She said the owners were asking an absurd price. She thought eighteen guineas a week for a house out in the country and miles from anywhere was ridiculous. I thought so too.'

'Yes, that is extraordinary, very extraordinary,' Clarissa agreed, with a friendly smile. 'I understand why you were sceptical. But perhaps now you'll believe some of the other things I said.'

'I'm not doubting your final story, Mrs Hailsham-Brown,' the Inspector assured her. 'We usually know the truth when we hear it. I knew, too, that there would have to be some serious reason for those three gentlemen to cook up this harebrained scheme of concealment.'

'You mustn't blame them too much, Inspector,' Clarissa pleaded. 'It was my fault. I went on and on at them.'

All too aware of her charm, the Inspector replied, 'Ah, I've no doubt you did. But what I still don't understand is, who telephoned the police in the first place and reported the murder?'

'Yes, that is extraordinary!' said Clarissa, sounding startled.

'I'd completely forgotten that.'

'It clearly wasn't you,' the Inspector pointed out, 'and it wouldn't have been any of the three gentlemen — '

Clarissa shook her head. 'Could it have been Elgin?' she wondered. 'Or perhaps Miss Peake?'

'I don't think it could possibly have been Miss Peake,' said the Inspector. 'She clearly didn't know Costello's body was there.'

'I wonder if that's so,' said Clarissa thoughtfully.

'After all, when the body was discovered, she had hysterics,' the Inspector reminded her.

'Oh, that's nothing. Anyone can have hysterics,' Clarissa remarked incautiously. The Inspector shot her a suspicious glance, at which she felt it expedient to give him as innocent a smile as she could manage.

'Anyway, Miss Peake doesn't live in the house,' the Inspector observed. 'She has her own cottage in the grounds.'

'But she could have been in the house,' said Clarissa. 'You know, she has keys to all the doors.'

The Inspector shook his head. 'No, it looks to me more like Elgin who must have called us,' he said.

Clarissa moved closer to him, and flashed him a somewhat anxious smile. 'You're not going to send me to prison, are you?' she asked. 'Uncle Roly said he was sure you wouldn't.'

The Inspector gave her an austere look. 'It's a good thing you changed your story in time, and told us the truth, madam,' he advised her sternly. 'But, if I may say so, Mrs Hailsham-Brown, I think you should get in touch with your solicitor as soon as possible and give him all the relevant facts. In the meantime, I'll get your statement typed out and read over to you, and perhaps you will be good enough to sign it.'

Clarissa was about to reply when the hall door opened and Sir Rowland entered. 'I couldn't keep away any longer,' he explained. 'Is it all right now, Inspector? Do you understand what our dilemma was?'

Clarissa went across to her guardian before he could say any more. 'Roly, darling,' she greeted him, taking his hand. 'I've made a statement, and the police — or rather Mr Jones here — is going to type it out. Then I've got to sign it, and I've told them everything.'

The Inspector went over to confer with the Constable, and Clarissa continued speaking quietly to Sir Rowland. 'I told them how I thought it was a burglar,' she said with emphasis, 'and hit him on the head — '

When Sir Rowland looked at her in alarm and opened his mouth to speak, she quickly covered his mouth with her hands so that he could not get the words out. She continued hurriedly, 'Then I told them how it turned out to be Oliver Costello, and how I got in a terrible flap and rang you, and how I begged and begged and at last you all gave in. I see now how wrong of me it was — '

The Inspector turned back to them, and Clarissa removed her hand from Sir Rowland's mouth just in time. 'But when it happened,' she was saying, 'I was just scared stiff, and I thought it would be cosier for everybody — me, Henry and even Miranda — if Oliver was found in Marsden Wood.'

Sir Rowland looked aghast. 'Clarissa! What on earth have you been saying?' he gasped.

'Mrs Hailsham-Brown has made a very full statement, sir,' the Inspector said complacently.

Recovering himself somewhat, Sir Rowland replied drily, 'So it seems.'

'It's the best thing to do,' said Clarissa. 'In fact, it was the only thing to do. The Inspector made me see that. And I'm truly sorry to have told all those silly lies.'

'It will lead to far less trouble in the end,' the Inspector assured her. 'Now, Mrs Hailsham-Brown,' he went on, 'I shan't ask you to go into the recess while the body is still there, but I'd like you to show me exactly where the man was standing when you came through that way into this room.'

'Oh — yes — well — he was — ' Clarissa began hesitantly. She went across to the desk. 'No,' she continued, 'I remember now. He was standing here like this.' She stood at one end of the desk, and leaned over it.

'Be ready to open the panel when I give you the word, Jones,' said the Inspector, motioning to the Constable, who rose and put his hand on the panel switch.

'I see,' the Inspector said to Clarissa. 'That's where he was standing. And then the door opened and you came out. All right, I don't want you to have to look in there at the body now, so just stand in front of the panel when it opens. Now — Jones.'

The Constable activated the switch, and the panel opened. The recess was empty except for a small piece of paper on the floor which Constable Jones retrieved, while the Inspector looked accusingly at Clarissa and Sir Rowland.

The Constable read out what was on the slip of paper. 'Sucks to you!' As the Inspector snatched the paper from him, Clarissa and Sir Rowland looked at each other in astonishment.

A loud ring from the front-door bell broke the silence.

19

A few moments later Elgin came into the drawing-room to announce that the Divisional Surgeon had arrived. The Inspector and Constable Jones immediately accompanied the butler to the front door, where the Inspector had the unenviable task of confessing to the Divisional Surgeon that, as it turned out, there was at present no body to examine.

'Really, Inspector Lord,' the Divisional Surgeon said irritably. 'Do you realize how infuriating it is to have brought me all this way on a wild-goose chase?'

'But I assure you, Doctor,' the Inspector attempted to explain, 'we did have a body.'

'The Inspector's right, Doctor,' Constable Jones added his voice. 'We certainly did have a body. It just happens to have disappeared.'

The sound of their voices had brought Hugo and Jeremy out from the dining-room on the other side of the hall. They could not refrain from making unhelpful comments. 'I can't think how you policemen ever get anything done — losing bodies indeed,' Hugo expostulated, while Jeremy exclaimed, 'I don't understand why a guard wasn't put on the body.'

'Well, whatever has happened, if there's no body for me to examine, I'm not wasting any more time here,' the Divisional Surgeon snapped at the Inspector. 'I can assure you that you'll hear more about this, Inspector Lord.'

'Yes, Doctor. I've no doubt of that. Goodnight, Doctor,' the Inspector replied wearily.

The Divisional Surgeon left, slamming the front door behind him, and the Inspector turned to Elgin, who forestalled him by saying quickly, 'I know nothing about it, I assure you, sir, nothing at all.'

Meanwhile, in the drawing-room, Clarissa and Sir Rowland were enjoying overhearing the discomfiture of the police officers. 'Rather a bad moment for the police reinforcements to arrive,' Sir Rowland chuckled. 'The Divisional Surgeon seems very annoyed at finding no corpse to examine.'

Clarissa giggled. 'But who can have spirited it away?' she asked. 'Do you think Jeremy managed it somehow?'

'I don't see how he could have done,' Sir Rowland replied. 'They didn't let anyone back into the library, and the door from the library to the hall was locked. Pippa's 'Sucks to you' was the last straw.'

Clarissa laughed, and Sir Rowland continued, 'Still, it shows us one thing. Costello had
managed to open the secret drawer.' He
paused, and his manner changed. 'Clarissa,'
he said in a serious tone, 'why on earth didn't
you tell the truth to the Inspector when I
begged you to?'

'I did,' Clarissa protested, 'except for the
part about Pippa. But he just didn't believe
me.'

'But, for Heaven's sake, why did you have
to stuff him with all that nonsense?' Sir
Rowland insisted on knowing.

'Well,' Clarissa replied with a helpless
gesture, 'it seemed to me the most likely thing
he would believe. And,' she ended trium-
phantly, 'he does believe me now.'

'And a nice mess you're in as a result,' Sir
Rowland pointed out. 'You'll be up on a
charge of manslaughter, for all you know.'

'I shall claim it was self-defence,' Clarissa
said confidently.

Before Sir Rowland had a chance to reply,
Hugo and Jeremy entered from the hall,
and Hugo walked over to the bridge table,
grumbling. 'Wretched police, pushing us
around here and there. Now it seems they've
gone and lost the body.'

Jeremy closed the door behind him, then
went over to the stool and took a sandwich.

'Damn peculiar, I call it,' he announced.

'It's fantastic,' said Clarissa. 'The whole thing's fantastic. The body's gone, and we still don't know who rang up the police in the first place and said there'd been a murder here.'

'Well, that was Elgin, surely,' Jeremy suggested, as he sat on an arm of the sofa and began to eat his sandwich.

'No, no,' Hugo disagreed. 'I'd say it was that Peake woman.'

'But why?' Clarissa asked. 'Why would either of them do that, and not tell us? It doesn't make sense.'

Miss Peake put her head in at the hall door and looked around with a conspiratorial air. 'Hello, is the coast clear?' she asked. Closing the door, she strode confidently into the room. 'No bobbies about? They seem to be swarming all over the place.'

'They're busy searching the house and grounds now,' Sir Rowland informed her.

'What for?' asked Miss Peake.

'The body,' Sir Rowland replied. 'It's gone.'

Miss Peake gave her usual hearty laugh. 'What a lark!' she boomed. 'The disappearing body, eh?'

Hugo sat at the bridge table. Looking around the room, he observed to no one in particular, 'It's a nightmare. The whole thing's a damn nightmare.'

'Quite like the movies, eh, Mrs Hailsham-Brown?' Miss Peake suggested with another hoot of laughter.

Sir Rowland smiled at the gardener. 'I hope you are feeling better now, Miss Peake?' he asked her courteously.

'Oh, I'm all right,' she replied. 'I'm pretty tough really, you know. I was just a bit bowled over by opening that door and finding a corpse. Turned me up for the moment, I must admit.'

'I wondered, perhaps,' said Clarissa quietly, 'if you already knew it was there.'

The gardener stared at her. 'Who? Me?'
'Yes. You.'

Again seeming to be addressing the entire universe, Hugo said, 'It doesn't make sense. Why take the body away? We all know there is a body. We know his identity and everything. No point in it. Why not leave the wretched thing where it was?'

'Oh, I wouldn't say there was no point in it, Mr Birch,' Miss Peake corrected Hugo, leaning across the bridge table to address him. 'You've got to have a body, you know. Habeas corpus and all that. Remember? You've got to have a body before you can bring a charge of murder against anybody.' She turned around to Clarissa. 'So don't you worry, Mrs Hailsham-Brown,' she assured

183

her. 'Everything's going to be all right.'

Clarissa stared at her. 'What do you mean?'

'I've kept my ears open this evening,' the gardener told her. 'I haven't spent all my time lying on the bed in the spare room.' She looked around at everyone. 'I never liked that man Elgin, or his wife,' she continued. 'Listening at doors, and running to the police with stories about blackmail.'

'So you heard that?' Clarissa asked, wonderingly.

'What I always say is, stand by your own sex,' Miss Peake declared. She looked at Hugo. 'Men!' she snorted. 'I don't hold with them.' She sat down next to Clarissa on the sofa. 'If they can't find the body, my dear,' she explained, 'they can't bring a charge against you. And what I say is, if that brute was blackmailing you, you did quite right to crack him over the head and good riddance.'

'But I didn't — ' Clarissa began faintly, only to be interrupted by Miss Peake.

'I heard you tell that Inspector all about it,' the gardener informed her. 'And if it wasn't for that eavesdropping skulking fellow Elgin, your story would sound quite all right. Perfectly believable.'

'Which story do you mean?' Clarissa wondered aloud.

'About mistaking him for a burglar. It's the

blackmail angle that puts a different complexion on it all. So I thought there was only one thing to do,' the gardener continued. 'Get rid of the body and let the police chase their tails looking for it.'

Sir Rowland took a few steps backward, staggering in disbelief, as Miss Peake looked complacently around the room. 'Pretty smart work, even if I do say so myself,' she boasted.

Jeremy rose, fascinated. 'Do you mean to say that it was you who moved the body?' he asked, incredulously.

Everyone was now staring at Miss Peake. 'We're all friends here, aren't we?' she asked, looking around at them. 'So I may as well spill the beans. Yes,' she admitted, 'I moved the body.' She tapped her pocket. 'And I locked the door. I've got keys to all the doors in this house, so that was no problem.'

Open-mouthed, Clarissa gazed at her in wonderment. 'But how? Where — where did you put the body?' she gasped.

Miss Peake leaned forward and spoke in a conspiratorial whisper. 'The bed in the spare room. You know, that big four-poster. Right across the head of the bed, under the bolster. Then I remade the bed and lay down on top of it.'

Sir Rowland, flabbergasted, sat down at the bridge table.

'But how did you get the body up to the spare room?' Clarissa asked. 'You couldn't manage it all by yourself.'

'You'd be surprised,' said Miss Peake jovially. 'Good old fireman's lift. Slung it over my shoulder.' With a gesture, she demonstrated how it was done.

'But what if you had met someone on the stairs?' Sir Rowland asked her.

'Ah, but I didn't,' replied Miss Peake. 'The police were in here with Mrs Hailsham-Brown. You three chaps were being kept in the dining-room by then. So I grabbed my chance, and of course grabbed the body too, took it through the hall, locked the library door again, and carried it up the stairs to the spare room.'

'Well, upon my soul!' Sir Rowland gasped.

Clarissa got to her feet. 'But he can't stay under the bolster for ever,' she pointed out.

Miss Peake turned to her. 'No, not for ever, of course, Mrs Hailsham-Brown,' she admitted. 'But he'll be all right for twenty-four hours. By that time, the police will have finished with the house and grounds. They'll be searching further afield.'

She looked around at her enthralled audience. 'Now, I've been thinking about how to get rid of him,' she went on. 'I happened to dig out a nice deep trench in the garden this morning — for the sweet peas. Well, we'll bury the body there and plant a nice double row of sweet peas all along it.'

Completely at a loss for words, Clarissa collapsed onto the sofa.

'I'm afraid, Miss Peake,' said Sir Rowland, 'grave-digging is no longer a matter for private enterprise.'

The gardener laughed merrily at this. 'Oh, you men!' she exclaimed, wagging her finger at Sir Rowland. 'Always such sticklers for propriety. We women have got more common sense.' She turned to address Clarissa. 'We can even take murder in our stride. Eh, Mrs Hailsham-Brown?'

Hugo suddenly leapt to his feet. 'This is absurd!' he shouted. 'Clarissa didn't kill him. I don't believe a word of it.'

'Well, if she didn't kill him,' Miss Peake asked breezily, 'who did?'

At that moment, Pippa entered the room from the hall, wearing a dressing-gown, walking in a very sleepy manner, yawning, and carrying a glass dish containing chocolate mousse with a teaspoon in it. Everyone turned and looked at her.

20

Startled, Clarissa jumped to her feet. 'Pippa!'
she cried. 'What are you doing out of bed?'

'I woke up, so I came down,' said Pippa
between yawns.

Clarissa led her to the sofa. 'I'm so
frightfully hungry,' Pippa complained, yawning again. She sat, then looked up at Clarissa
and said, reproachfully, 'You said you'd bring
this up to me.'

Clarissa took the dish of chocolate mousse
from Pippa, placed it on the stool, and then
sat on the sofa next to the child. 'I thought
you were still asleep, Pippa,' she explained.

'I was asleep,' Pippa told her, with another
enormous yawn. 'Then I thought a policeman
came in and looked at me. I'd been having an
awful dream, and then I half woke up. Then I
was hungry, so I thought I'd come down.'

She shivered, looked around at everyone,
and continued, 'Besides, I thought it might be
true.'

Sir Rowland came and sat on the sofa on
Pippa's other side. 'What might be true,
Pippa?' he asked her.

'That horrible dream I had about Oliver,'

Pippa replied, shuddering as she recollected it.

'What was your dream about Oliver, Pippa?' Sir Rowland asked quietly. 'Tell me.'

Pippa looked nervous as she took a small piece of moulded wax from a pocket of her dressing-gown. 'I made this earlier tonight,' she said. 'I melted down a wax candle, then I made a pin red hot, and I stuck the pin through it.'

As she handed the small wax figure to Sir Rowland, Jeremy suddenly gave a startled exclamation of 'Good Lord!' He leapt up and began to look around the room, searching for the book Pippa had tried to show him earlier.

'I said the right words and everything,' Pippa was explaining to Sir Rowland, 'but I couldn't do it quite the way the book said.'

'What book?' Clarissa asked. 'I don't understand.'

Jeremy, who had been looking along the bookshelves, now found what he was seeking. 'Here it is,' he exclaimed, handing the book to Clarissa over the back of the sofa. 'Pippa got it in the market today. She called it a recipe book.'

Pippa suddenly laughed. 'And you said to me, 'Can you eat it?'' she reminded Jeremy.

Clarissa examined the book. '*A Hundred Well-tried and Trusty Spells*,' she read on the

189

cover. She opened the book, and read on. ''How to cure warts. How to get your heart's desire. How to destroy your enemy.' Oh, Pippa — is that what you did?'

Pippa looked at her stepmother solemnly. 'Yes,' she answered.

As Clarissa handed the book back to Jeremy, Pippa looked at the wax figure Sir Rowland was still holding. 'It isn't very like Oliver,' she admitted, 'and I couldn't get any clippings of his hair. But it was as much like him as I could make it — and then — then — I dreamed, I thought — ' She pushed her hair back from her face as she spoke. 'I thought I came down here and he was there.' She pointed behind the sofa. 'And it was all true.'

Sir Rowland put the wax figure down on the stool quietly, as Pippa continued, 'He was there, dead. I had killed him.' She looked around at them all, and began to shake. 'Is it true?' she asked. 'Did I kill him?'

'No, darling. No,' said Clarissa tearfully, putting an arm around Pippa.

'But he was there,' Pippa insisted.

'I know, Pippa,' Sir Rowland told her. 'But you didn't kill him. When you stuck the pin through that wax figure, it was your hate and your fear of him that you killed in that way. You're not afraid of him and you don't hate him any longer. Isn't that true?'

Pippa turned to him. 'Yes, it's true,' she admitted. 'But I did see him.' She glanced over the back of the sofa. 'I came down here and I saw him lying there, dead.' She leaned her head on Sir Rowland's chest. 'I did see him, Uncle Roly.'

'Yes, dear, you did see him,' Sir Rowland told her gently. 'But it wasn't you who killed him.' She looked up at him anxiously, and he continued, 'Now, listen to me, Pippa. Somebody hit him over the head with a big stick. You didn't do that, did you?'

'Oh, no,' said Pippa, shaking her head vigorously. 'No, not a stick.' She turned to Clarissa. 'You mean a golf stick like Jeremy had?'

Jeremy laughed. 'No, not a golf club, Pippa,' he explained. 'Something like that big stick that's kept in the hall stand.'

'You mean the one that used to belong to Mr Sellon, the one Miss Peake calls a knobkerry?' Pippa asked.

Jeremy nodded.

'Oh, no,' Pippa told him. 'I wouldn't do anything like that. I couldn't.' She turned back to Sir Rowland. 'Oh, Uncle Roly, I wouldn't have killed him really.'

'Of course you wouldn't,' Clarissa intervened in a voice of calm common-sense. 'Now come along, darling, you eat up your chocolate mousse and forget all about it.' She picked up the dish and offered it, but Pippa refused with a shake of her head, and Clarissa replaced the dish on the stool. She and Sir Rowland helped Pippa to lie down on the sofa, Clarissa took Pippa's hand, and Sir Rowland stroked the child's hair affectionately.

'I don't understand a word of all this,' Miss Peake announced. 'What is that book, anyway?' she asked Jeremy who was now glancing through it.

'"How to bring a murrain on your neighbour's cattle." Does that attract you, Miss Peake?' he replied. 'I daresay with a little adjusting you could bring black spot to your neighbour's roses.'

'I don't know what you're talking about,' the gardener said brusquely.

'Black magic,' Jeremy explained.

'I'm not superstitious, thank goodness,' she snorted dismissively, moving away from him.

Hugo, who had been attempting to follow the train of events, now confessed, 'I'm in a complete fog.'

'Me, too,' Miss Peake agreed, tapping him on the shoulder. 'So I'll just have a peep and see how the boys in blue are getting on.' With another of her boisterous laughs, she went out into the hall.

Sir Rowland looked around at Clarissa, Hugo and Jeremy. 'Now where does that leave us?' he wondered aloud.

Clarissa was still recovering from the revelations of the previous few minutes.

'What a fool I've been,' she exclaimed, confusedly. 'I should have known Pippa couldn't possibly — I didn't know anything about this book. Pippa said she killed him and I — I thought it was true.'

Hugo got to his feet. 'Oh, you mean that you thought Pippa — '

'Yes, darling,' Clarissa interrupted him urgently and emphatically to stop him from saying any more. But Pippa, fortunately, was now sleeping peacefully on the sofa.

'Oh, I see,' said Hugo. 'That explains it. Good God!'

'Well, we'd better go to the police now, and tell them the truth at last,' Jeremy suggested.

Sir Rowland shook his head thoughtfully. 'I don't know,' he murmured. 'Clarissa has already told them three different stories — '

'No. Wait,' Clarissa interrupted suddenly. 'I've just had an idea. Hugo, what was the name of Mr Sellon's shop?'

'It was just an antique shop,' Hugo replied, vaguely.

'Yes, I know that,' Clarissa exclaimed impatiently. 'But what was it called?'

'What do you mean — 'what was it called'?'

'Oh, dear, you are being difficult,' Clarissa told him. 'You said it earlier, and I want you to say it again. But I don't want to tell you to say it, or say it for you.'

Hugo, Jeremy and Sir Rowland all looked at one another. 'Do you know what the blazes the girl is getting at, Roly?' Hugo asked plaintively.

'I've no idea,' replied Sir Rowland. 'Try us again, Clarissa.'

Clarissa looked exasperated. 'It's perfectly simple,' she insisted. 'What was the name of the antique shop in Maidstone?'

'It hadn't got a name,' Hugo replied. 'I mean, antique shops aren't called 'Seaview' or anything.'

'Heaven give me patience,' Clarissa muttered between clenched teeth. Speaking slowly and distinctly, and pausing after each word, she asked him again, 'What — was — written — up — over — the — door?'

'Written up? Nothing,' said Hugo. 'What should be written up? Only the names of the owners, 'Sellon and Brown', of course.'

'At last,' Clarissa cried jubilantly. 'I thought that was what you said before, but I wasn't sure. Sellon and Brown. My name is Hailsham-Brown.' She looked at the three men in turn, but they merely stared back at her with total incomprehension written on their faces.

'We got this house dirt cheap,' Clarissa continued. 'Other people who came to see it before us were asked such an exorbitant rent that they went away in disgust. Now have you got it?'

Hugo looked at her blankly before replying, 'No.'

Jeremy shook his head. 'Not yet, my love.'

Sir Rowland looked at her keenly. 'In a glass darkly,' he said thoughtfully.

Clarissa's face wore a look of intense excitement. 'Mr Sellon's partner who lives in London is a woman,' she explained to her friends. 'Today, someone rang up here and asked to speak to Mrs Brown. Not Mrs Hailsham-Brown, just Mrs Brown.'

'I see what you're getting at,' Sir Rowland said, nodding his head slowly.

Hugo shook his head. 'I don't,' he admitted.

Clarissa looked at him. 'A horse chestnut or a chestnut horse — one of them makes all the difference,' she observed inscrutably.

'You're not delirious or anything, are you, Clarissa?' Hugo asked her anxiously.

'Somebody killed Oliver,' Clarissa reminded them. 'It wasn't any of you three. It wasn't me or Henry.' She paused, before continuing, 'And it wasn't Pippa, thank God. Then who was it?'

'Surely it's as I said to the Inspector,' Sir Rowland suggested. 'An outside job. Someone followed Oliver here.'

'Yes, but why did they?' Clarissa asked meaningfully. Getting no reply from anyone, she continued with her speculation. 'When I left you all at the gate today,' she reminded her three friends, 'I came back in through the French windows, and Oliver was standing here. He was very surprised to see me. He said, 'What are you doing here, Clarissa?' I just thought it was an elaborate way of annoying me. But suppose it was just what it seemed?'

Her hearers looked attentive, but said nothing. Clarissa continued, 'Just suppose that he was surprised to see me. He thought the house belonged to someone else. He thought the person he'd find here would be the Mrs Brown who was Mr Sellon's partner.'

Sir Rowland shook his head. 'Wouldn't he know that you and Henry had this house?' he asked her. 'Wouldn't Miranda know?'

'When Miranda has to communicate, she always does it through her lawyers. Neither she nor Oliver necessarily knew that we lived in this house,' Clarissa explained. 'I tell you, I'm sure Oliver Costello had no idea he was going to see me. Oh, he recovered pretty quickly and made the excuse that he'd come to talk about Pippa. Then he pretended to go away, but he came back because — '

She broke off as Miss Peake came in through the hall door. 'The hunt's still on,' the gardener announced briskly. 'They've looked under all the beds, I gather, and now they're out in the grounds.' She gave her familiar hearty laugh.

Clarissa looked at her keenly. Then, 'Miss Peake,' she said, 'do you remember what Mr Costello said just before he left? Do you?'

Miss Peake looked blank. 'Haven't the foggiest idea,' she admitted.

'He said, didn't he, 'I came to see Mrs Brown'?' Clarissa reminded her.

Miss Peake thought for a moment, and then answered, 'I believe he did. Yes. Why?'

'But it wasn't me he came to see,' Clarissa insisted.

'Well, if it wasn't you, then I don't know who it could have been,' Miss Peake replied with another of her jovial laughs.

Clarissa spoke with emphasis. 'It was you,' she said to the gardener. '*You* are Mrs Brown, aren't you?'

21

Miss Peake, looking extremely startled at Clarissa's accusation, seemed for a moment unsure how to act. When she did reply, her manner had changed. Dropping her usual jolly, hearty tone, she spoke gravely. 'That's very bright of you,' she said. 'Yes, I'm Mrs Brown.'

Clarissa had been doing some quick thinking. 'You're Mr Sellon's partner,' she said. 'You own this house. You inherited it from Sellon with the business. For some reason, you had the idea of finding a tenant for it whose name was Brown. In fact, you were determined to have a Mrs Brown in residence here. You thought that wouldn't be too difficult, since it's such a common name. But in the end you had to compromise on Hailsham-Brown. I don't know exactly why you wanted me to be in the limelight whilst you watched. I don't understand the ins and outs — '

Mrs Brown, alias Miss Peake, interrupted her. 'Charles Sellon was murdered,' she told Clarissa. 'There's no doubt of that. He'd got hold of something that was very valuable. I don't know how — I don't even know what it was. He wasn't always very — ' she hesitated ' — scrupulous.'

'So we have heard,' Sir Rowland observed drily.

'Whatever it was,' Mrs Brown continued, 'he was killed for it. And whoever killed him didn't find the thing. That was probably because it wasn't in the shop, it was here. I thought that whoever it was who killed him would come here sooner or later, looking for it. I wanted to be on the watch, therefore I needed a dummy Mrs Brown. A substitute.'

Sir Rowland made an exclamation of annoyance. 'It didn't worry you,' he asked the gardener, speaking with feeling, 'that Mrs Hailsham-Brown, a perfectly innocent woman who had done you no harm, would be in danger?'

'I've kept an eye on her, haven't I?' Mrs Brown replied defensively. 'So much so that it annoyed you all sometimes. The other day, when a man came along and offered her a ridiculous price for that desk, I was sure I was on the right track. Yet I'll swear there was nothing in that desk that meant anything at all.'

'Did you examine the secret drawer?' Sir Rowland asked her.

Mrs Brown looked surprised. 'A secret drawer, is there?' she exclaimed, moving towards the desk.

Clarissa intercepted her. 'There's nothing there now,' she assured her. 'Pippa found the drawer, but there were only some old autographs in it.'

'Clarissa, I'd rather like to see those autographs again,' Sir Rowland requested.

Clarissa went to the sofa. 'Pippa,' she called, 'where did you put — ? Oh, she's asleep.'

Mrs Brown moved to the sofa and looked down at the child. 'Fast asleep,' she confirmed. 'It's all the excitement that's done that.' She looked at Clarissa. 'I'll tell you what,' she said, 'I'll carry her up and dump her on her bed.'

'No,' said Sir Rowland, sharply.

Everyone looked at him. 'She's no weight at all,' Mrs Brown pointed out. 'Not a quarter as heavy as the late Mr Costello.'

'All the same,' Sir Rowland insisted, 'I think she'll be safer here.'

The others now all looked at Miss Peake/Mrs Brown, who took a step backwards, looked around her, and exclaimed indignantly, 'Safer?'

'That's what I said,' Sir Rowland told her. He glanced around the room, and continued, 'That child said a very significant thing just now.'

He sat down at the bridge table, watched

by all. There was a pause, and then Hugo, moving to sit opposite Sir Rowland at the bridge table, asked, 'What did she say, Roly?'

'If you all think back,' Sir Rowland suggested, 'perhaps you'll realize what it was.'

His hearers looked at one another, while Sir Rowland picked up the copy of *Who's Who* and began to consult it.

'I don't get it,' Hugo admitted, shaking his head.

'What did Pippa say?' Jeremy wondered aloud.

'I can't imagine,' said Clarissa. She tried to cast her mind back. 'Something about the policeman? Or dreaming? Coming down here? Half awake?'

'Come on, Roly,' Hugo urged his friend. 'Don't be so damned mysterious. What's this all about?'

Sir Rowland looked up. 'What?' he asked, absent-mindedly. 'Oh, yes. Those autographs. Where are they?'

Hugo snapped his fingers. 'I believe I remember Pippa putting them in that shell box over there,' he recalled.

Jeremy went over to the bookshelves. 'Up here?' he asked. Locating the shell box, he took out the envelope. 'Yes, quite right. Here we are,' he confirmed as he took the autographs from the envelope and handed them to Sir Rowland, who had now closed *Who's Who*. Jeremy put the empty envelope in his pocket while Sir Rowland examined the autographs with his eyeglass.

'Victoria Regina, God bless her,' murmured Sir Rowland, looking at the first of the autographs. 'Queen Victoria. Faded brown ink. Now, what's this one? John Ruskin — yes, that's authentic, I should say. And this one? Robert Browning — Hm — the paper's not as old as it ought to be.'

'Roly! What do you mean?' Clarissa asked excitedly.

'I had some experience of invisible inks and that sort of thing, during the war,' Sir Rowland explained. 'If you wanted to make a secret note of something, it wouldn't be a bad idea to write it in invisible ink on a sheet of paper, and then fake an autograph. Put that autograph with other genuine autographs and nobody would notice it or look at it twice, probably. Any more than we did.'

Mrs Brown looked puzzled. 'But what could Charles Sellon have written which would be worth fourteen thousand pounds?' she wanted to know.

'Nothing at all, dear lady,' Sir Rowland replied. 'But it occurs to me, you know, that it might have been a question of safety.'

'Safety?' Mrs Brown queried.

'Oliver Costello,' Sir Rowland explained, 'is suspected of supplying drugs. Sellon, so the Inspector tells us, was questioned once or twice by the Narcotics Squad. There's a connection there, don't you think?'

When Mrs Brown merely looked blank, he continued, 'Of course, it might be just a foolish idea of mine.' He looked down at the autograph he was holding. 'I don't think it would be anything elaborate on Sellon's part. Lemon juice, perhaps, or a solution of barium chloride. Gentle heat might do the trick. We can always try iodine vapour later. Yes, let's try a little gentle heat first.'

He rose to his feet. 'Shall we attempt the experiment?'

'There's an electric fire in the library,' Clarissa remembered. 'Jeremy, will you get it?'

Hugo rose and tucked in his chair, while Jeremy went off to the library.

'We can plug it in here,' Clarissa pointed out, indicating a socket in the skirting-board running around the drawing-room.

'The whole thing's ridiculous,' Mrs Brown snorted. 'It's too far-fetched for words.'

Clarissa disagreed. 'No, it isn't. I think it's a wonderful idea,' she declared, as Jeremy returned from the library carrying a small electric radiator. 'Got it?' she asked him.

'Here it is,' he replied. 'Where's the plug?'

'Down there,' Clarissa told him, pointing. She held the radiator while Jeremy plugged its lead into the socket, and then she put it down on the floor.

Sir Rowland took the Robert Browning autograph and stood close to the radiator. Jeremy knelt by it, and the others stood as close as possible to observe the result.

'We mustn't hope for too much,' Sir Rowland warned them. 'After all, it's only an idea of mine, but there must have been some very good reason why Sellon kept these bits of paper in such a secret place.'

'This takes me back years,' Hugo recalled. 'I remember writing secret messages with lemon juice when I was a kid.'

'Which one shall we start with?' Jeremy asked enthusiastically.

'I say Queen Victoria,' said Clarissa.

'No, six to one on Ruskin,' was Jeremy's guess.

'Well, I'm putting my money on Robert Browning,' Sir Rowland decided, bending over and holding the paper in front of the radiator.

'Ruskin? Most obscure chap. I never could understand a word of his poetry,' Hugo felt moved to comment.

'Exactly,' Sir Rowland agreed. 'It's full of hidden meaning.'

They all craned over Sir Rowland. 'I can't bear it if nothing happens,' Clarissa exclaimed.

'I believe — yes, there's something there,' Sir Rowland murmured.

'Yes, there is something coming up,' Jeremy noticed.

'Is there? Let me see,' said Clarissa excitedly.

Hugo pushed between Clarissa and Jeremy. 'Out of the way, young man.'

'Steady,' Sir Rowland complained. 'Don't joggle me — yes — there is writing.' He paused for a moment, and then straightened up with a cry of, 'We've got it!'

'What have you got?' Mrs Brown wanted to know.

'A list of six names and addresses,' Sir Rowland told them. 'Distributors in the drug racket, I should say. And one of those names is Oliver Costello.'

There were exclamations all around. 'Oliver!' said Clarissa. 'So that's why he came, and someone must have followed him and — Oh, Uncle Roly, we must tell the police. Come along, Hugo.'

Clarissa rushed to the hall door followed by Hugo who, as he went, was muttering, 'Most extraordinary thing I ever heard of.' Sir Rowland picked up the other autographs, while Jeremy unplugged the radiator and took it back into the library.

About to follow Clarissa and Hugo out, Sir Rowland paused in the doorway. 'Coming, Miss Peake?' he asked.

'You don't need me, do you?'

'I think we do. You were Sellon's partner.'

'I've never had anything to do with the drug business,' Mrs Brown insisted. 'I just ran the antique side. I did all the London buying and selling.'

'I see,' Sir Rowland replied non-committally as he held the hall door open for her.

Jeremy returned from the library, closing the door carefully behind him. He went over to the hall door and listened for a moment. After a glance at Pippa, he went over to the easy chair, picked up the cushion from it, and moved slowly back towards the sofa where Pippa lay sleeping.

Pippa stirred in her sleep. Jeremy stood frozen for a moment, but when he was certain she was still asleep, he continued towards the sofa until he stood behind Pippa's head. Then, slowly, he began to lower the cushion over her face.

At that moment, Clarissa re-entered the room from the hall. Hearing the door, Jeremy carefully placed the cushion over Pippa's feet. 'I remembered what Sir Rowland said,' he explained to Clarissa, 'so I thought perhaps we oughtn't to leave Pippa all alone. Her feet seemed a bit cold, so I was just covering them up.'

Clarissa went across to the stool. 'All this excitement has made me feel terribly hungry,' she declared. She looked down at the plate of sandwiches, and then continued in a tone of great disappointment, 'Oh, Jeremy, you've eaten them all.'

'Sorry, but I was starving,' he said, sounding not at all sorry.

'I don't see why you should be,' she reprimanded him. 'You've had dinner. I haven't.'

Jeremy perched on the back of the sofa. 'No, I haven't had any dinner either,' he told her. 'I was practising approach shots. I only came into the dining-room just after your telephone call came.'

'Oh, I see,' Clarissa replied nonchalantly. She bent over the back of the sofa to pat the cushion. Suddenly her eyes widened. In a deeply moved voice she repeated, 'I see. You — it was you.'

'What do you mean?'

'You!' Clarissa repeated, almost to herself.

'What do you mean?'

Clarissa looked him in the eye. 'What were you doing with that cushion when I came into the room?' she asked.

He laughed. 'I told you. I was covering up Pippa's feet. They were cold.'

'Were you? Is that really what you were going to do? Or were you going to put that cushion over her mouth?'

'Clarissa!' he exclaimed indignantly. 'What a ridiculous thing to say!'

'I was certain that none of us could have killed Oliver Costello. I said so to everyone,' Clarissa recalled. 'But one of us could have killed him. You. You were out on the golf course alone. You could have come back to the house, got in through the library window which you'd left open, and you had your golf club still in your hand. Of course. That's what Pippa saw. That's what she meant when she said, 'A golf stick like Jeremy had'. She saw you.'

'That's absolute nonsense, Clarissa,' Jeremy objected, with a poor attempt at a laugh.

'No, it isn't,' she insisted. 'Then, after you'd killed Oliver you went back to the club and rang the police so that they would come here, find the body, and think it was Henry or I who had killed him.'

Jeremy leaped to his feet. 'What bloody rubbish!' he declared.

'It's not rubbish. It's true. I know it's true,' Clarissa exclaimed. 'But why? That's what I don't understand. Why?'

They stood facing each other in tense silence for a few moments. Then Jeremy gave a deep sigh. He took from his pocket the envelope that had contained the autographs. He held it out to Clarissa, but did not let her take it. 'This is what it's all about,' he told her.

Clarissa glanced at it. 'That's the envelope the autographs were kept in,' she said.

'There's a stamp on it,' Jeremy explained quietly. 'It's what's known as an error stamp. Printed in the wrong colour. One from Sweden sold last year for fourteen thousand three hundred pounds.'

'So that's it,' Clarissa gasped, stepping backwards.

'This stamp came into Sellon's possession,' Jeremy continued. 'He wrote to my boss Sir Kenneth about it. But it was I who opened the letter. I came down here and visited Sellon — '

He paused, and Clarissa completed his sentence for him: ' — and killed him.'

Jeremy nodded without saying anything.

'But you couldn't find the stamp,' Clarissa guessed aloud, backing away from him.

'You're right again,' Jeremy admitted. 'It wasn't in the shop, so I felt sure it must be here, in his house.'

He began to move towards Clarissa, as she

continued to back away. 'Tonight I thought Costello had beaten me to it.'

'And so you killed him, too,' said Clarissa. Jeremy nodded again.

'And just now, you would have killed Pippa?' she gasped.

'Why not?' he replied blandly.

'I can't believe it,' Clarissa told him.

'My dear Clarissa, fourteen thousand pounds is a great deal of money,' he observed with a smile that contrived to be both apologetic and sinister.

'But why are you telling me this?' she asked, sounding both perplexed and anxious. 'Do you imagine for one moment that I shan't go to the police?'

'You've told them so many lies, they'll never believe you,' he replied off-handedly.

'Oh yes, they will.'

'Besides,' Jeremy continued, advancing upon her, 'you're not going to get the chance. Do you think that when I've killed two people I shall worry about killing a third?'

He gripped Clarissa by the throat, and she screamed.

22

Clarissa's scream was answered immediately. Sir Rowland came in swiftly from the hall, switching on the wall-brackets as he did so, while Constable Jones rushed into the room through the French windows, and the Inspector hurried in from the library.

The Inspector grabbed Jeremy. 'All right, Warrender. We've heard it all, thank you,' he announced. 'And that's just the evidence we need,' he added. 'Give me that envelope.'

Clarissa backed behind the sofa, holding her throat, and Jeremy handed the envelope to the Inspector, observing coolly, 'So it was a trap, was it? Very clever.'

'Jeremy Warrender,' said the Inspector, 'I arrest you for the murder of Oliver Costello, and I must warn you that anything you say may be taken down and given in evidence.'

'You can save your breath, Inspector,' was Jeremy's smoothly uttered reply. 'I'm not saying anything. It was a good gamble, but it just didn't work.'

'Take him away,' the Inspector instructed Constable Jones, who took Jeremy by the arm.

'What's the matter, Mr Jones? Forgotten your handcuffs?' Jeremy asked coldly as his right arm was twisted behind his back and he was marched off through the French windows.

Shaking his head sadly, Sir Rowland watched him go, and then turned to Clarissa. 'Are you all right, my dear?' he asked her anxiously.

'Yes, yes, I'm all right,' Clarissa replied somewhat breathlessly.

'I never meant to expose you to this,' Sir Rowland said apologetically.

She looked at him shrewdly. 'You knew it was Jeremy, didn't you?' she asked.

The Inspector added his voice. 'But what made you think of the stamp, sir?'

Sir Rowland approached Inspector Lord and took the envelope from him. 'Well, Inspector,' he began, 'it rang a bell when Pippa gave me the envelope this evening. Then, when I found from *Who's Who* that young Warrender's employer, Sir Kenneth Thomson, was a stamp collector, my suspicion developed, and just now, when he had the impertinence to pocket the envelope under my nose, I felt it was a certainty.'

He returned the envelope to the Inspector. 'Take great care of this, Inspector. You'll probably find it's extremely valuable, besides being evidence.'

'It's evidence, all right,' replied the Inspector. 'A particularly vicious young criminal is going to get his deserts.' Walking across to the hall door, he continued, 'However, we've still got to find the body.'

'Oh, that's easy, Inspector,' Clarissa assured him. 'Look in the bed in the spare room.'

The Inspector turned and regarded her disapprovingly. 'Now, really, Mrs Hailsham-Brown — ' he began.

He was interrupted by Clarissa. 'Why does nobody ever believe me?' she cried plaintively. 'It is in the spare room bed. You go and look, Inspector. Across the bed, under the bolster. Miss Peake put it there, trying to be kind.'

'Trying to be — ?' The Inspector broke off, clearly at a loss for words. He went to the door, turned, and said reproachfully, 'You know, Mrs Hailsham-Brown, you haven't made things easier for us tonight, telling us all these tall stories. I suppose you thought your husband had done it, and were lying to cover up for him. But you shouldn't do it, madam. You really shouldn't do it.' With a final shake of his head, he left the room.

'Well!' Clarissa exclaimed indignantly. She turned towards the sofa. 'Oh, Pippa — ' she remembered.

'Better get her up to bed,' Sir Rowland advised. 'She'll be safe now.'

Gently shaking the child, Clarissa said softly, 'Come on, Pippa. Ups-a-daisy. Time you were in bed.'

Pippa got up, waveringly. 'I'm hungry,' she murmured.

'Yes, yes, I'm sure you are,' Clarissa assured her as she led her to the hall door. 'Come on, we'll see what we can find.'

'Good night, Pippa,' Sir Rowland called to her, and was rewarded with a yawned 'Goo' night' as Clarissa and Pippa left the room. He sat down at the bridge table and had begun to put the playing cards in their boxes when Hugo came in from the hall.

'God bless my soul,' Hugo exclaimed. 'I'd never have believed it. Young Warrender, of all people. He seemed a decent enough young fellow. Been to a good school. Knew all the right people.'

'But was quite willing to commit murder for the sake of fourteen thousand pounds,' Sir Rowland observed suavely. 'It happens now and then, Hugo, in every class of society. An attractive personality, and no moral sense.'

Mrs Brown, the erstwhile Miss Peake, stuck her head around the hall door. 'I thought I'd just tell you, Sir Rowland,' she announced, reverting to her familiar booming voice, 'I've got to go along to the police station. They want me to make a statement.

214

They're not too pleased at the trick I played on them. I'm in for a wigging, I'm afraid.' She roared with laughter, withdrew, and slammed the door shut.

Hugo watched her go, then went over to join Sir Rowland at the bridge table. 'You know, Roly, I still don't quite get it,' he admitted. 'Was Miss Peake Mrs Sellon, or was Mr Sellon Mr Brown? Or the other way round?'

Sir Rowland was saved from having to reply by the return of the Inspector who came into the room to pick up his cap and gloves. 'We're removing the body now, gentlemen,' he informed them both. He paused momentarily before adding, 'Sir Rowland, would you mind advising Mrs Hailsham-Brown that, if she tells these fancy stories to the police, one day she'll get into real trouble.'

'She did actually tell you the truth once, you know, Inspector,' Sir Rowland reminded him gently, 'but on that occasion you simply wouldn't believe her.'

The Inspector looked a trifle embarrassed. 'Yes — hmmm — well,' he began. Then, pulling himself together, he said, 'Frankly, sir, it was a bit difficult to swallow, you'll admit.'

'Oh, I admit that, certainly,' Sir Rowland assured him.

'Not that I blame you, sir,' the Inspector

went on in a confidential tone. 'Mrs Hailsham-Brown is a lady who has a very taking way with her.' He shook his head reflectively, then, 'Well, good night, sir,' he said.

'Good night, Inspector,' Sir Rowland replied amiably.

'Good night, Mr Birch,' the Inspector called, backing towards the hall door.

'Good night, Inspector, and well done,' Hugo responded, coming over to him and shaking hands.

'Thank you, sir,' said the Inspector.

He left, and Hugo yawned. 'Oh, well, I suppose I'd better be going home to bed,' he announced to Sir Rowland. 'Some evening, eh?'

'As you say, Hugo, some evening,' Sir Rowland replied, tidying the bridge table as he spoke. 'Good night.'

'Good night,' Hugo responded, and made his way out into the hall.

Sir Rowland left the cards and markers in a neat pile on the table, then picked up *Who's Who* and replaced it on the bookshelves. Clarissa came in from the hall, went over to him and put her hands on his arms. 'Darling Roly,' she addressed him. 'What would we have done without you? You are so clever.'

'And you are a very lucky young woman,'

he told her. 'It's a good thing you didn't lose your heart to that young villain, Warrender.'

Clarissa shuddered. 'There was no danger of that,' she replied. Then, smiling tenderly, 'If I lost my heart to anybody, darling, it would be to you,' she assured him.

'Now, now, none of your tricks with me,' Sir Rowland warned her, laughing. 'If you — '

He stopped short as Henry Hailsham-Brown came in through the French windows, and Clarissa gave a startled exclamation. 'Henry!'

'Hello, Roly,' Henry greeted his friend. 'I thought you were going to the club tonight.'

'Well — er — I thought I'd turn in early,' was all that Sir Rowland felt capable of saying at that moment. 'It's been rather a strenuous evening.'

Henry looked at the bridge table. 'What? Strenuous bridge?' he inquired playfully.

Sir Rowland smiled. 'Bridge and — er — other things,' he replied as he went to the hall door. 'Good night, all.'

Clarissa blew him a kiss and he blew one to her in return as he left the room. Then Clarissa turned to Henry. 'Where's Kalendorff — I mean, where's Mr Jones?' she asked urgently.

Henry put his briefcase on the sofa. In a

voice of weary frustration he muttered, 'It's absolutely infuriating. He didn't come.'

'What?' Clarissa could hardly believe her ears.

'The plane arrived with nothing but a half-baked aide-de-camp in it,' Henry told her, unbuttoning his overcoat as he spoke.

Clarissa helped him off with the coat, and Henry continued, 'The first thing he did was to turn round and fly back again where he'd come from.'

'What on earth for?'

'How do I know?' Understandably, Henry sounded somewhat on edge. 'He was suspicious, it seems. Suspicious of what? Who knows?'

'But what about Sir John?' Clarissa asked as she removed Henry's hat from his head.

'That's the worst of it,' he groaned. 'I was too late to stop him, and he'll be arriving down here any minute now, I expect.' Henry consulted his watch. 'Of course, I rang up Downing Street at once from the aerodrome, but he'd already started out. Oh, the whole thing's a most ghastly fiasco.'

Henry sank on to the sofa with an exhausted sigh, and as he did so the telephone rang. 'I'll answer it,' Clarissa said, crossing the room to do so. 'It may be the police.' She lifted the receiver.

Henry looked at her questioningly. 'The police?'

'Yes, this is Copplestone Court,' Clarissa was saying into the telephone. 'Yes — yes, he's here.' She looked across at Henry. 'It's for you, darling,' she told him. 'It's Bindley Heath aerodrome.'

Henry rose and began to rush across to the phone, but stopped half-way and proceeded at a dignified walk. 'Hello,' he said into the receiver.

Clarissa took Henry's hat and coat to the hall but returned immediately and stood behind him.

'Yes — speaking,' Henry announced. 'What? — Ten minutes later? — Shall I? — Yes — Yes, yes — No — No, no — You have? — I see — Yes — Right.'

He replaced the receiver, shouted 'Clarissa!', and then turned to find that she was right behind him. 'Oh! There you are. Apparently another plane came in just ten minutes after the first, and Kalendorff was on it.'

'Mr Jones, you mean,' Clarissa reminded him.

'Quite right, darling. One can't be too careful,' he acknowledged. 'Yes, it seems that the first plane was a kind of security precaution. Really, one can't fathom how these people's minds work. Well, anyway, they're sending — er — Mr Jones over here now with an escort. He'll be here in about a quarter of an hour. Now then, is everything all right? Everything in order?' He looked at the bridge table. 'Do get rid of those cards, will you, darling?'

Clarissa hurriedly collected the cards and markers and put them out of sight, while Henry went to the stool and picked up the sandwich plate and mousse dish with an air of great surprise. 'What on earth's this?' he wanted to know.

Rushing over to him, Clarissa seized the plate and dish. 'Pippa was eating it,' she explained. 'I'll take it away. And I'd better go and make some more ham sandwiches.'

'Not yet — these chairs are all over the place.' Henry's tone was slightly reproachful. 'I thought you were going to have everything ready, Clarissa.'

He began to fold the legs of the bridge table. 'What have you been doing all the evening?' he asked her as he carried the bridge table off to the library.

Clarissa was now busy pushing chairs around. 'Oh, Henry,' she exclaimed, 'it's been the most terribly exciting evening. You see, I came in here with some sandwiches soon after you left, and the first thing that happened was I fell over a body. There.' She pointed. 'Behind the sofa.'

'Yes, yes, darling,' Henry muttered absent-mindedly, as he helped her push the easy chair into its usual position. 'Your stories are always enchanting, but really there isn't time now.'

'But, Henry, it's true,' she insisted. 'And that's only the beginning. The police came, and it was just one thing after another.' She was beginning to babble. 'There was a narcotic ring, and Miss Peake isn't Miss Peake, she's really Mrs Brown, and Jeremy turned out to be the murderer and he was trying to steal a stamp worth fourteen thousand pounds.'

'Hmm! Must have been a second Swedish yellow,' Henry commented. His tone was indulgent, but he was not really listening.

'I believe that's just what it was!' Clarissa exclaimed delightedly.

'Really, the things you imagine, Clarissa,' said Henry affectionately. He moved the small table, set it between the armchair and the easy chair, and flicked the crumbs off it with his handkerchief.

'But, darling, I didn't imagine it,' Clarissa went on. 'I couldn't have imagined half as much.'

Henry put his briefcase behind a cushion on the sofa, plumped up another cushion, then made his way with a third cushion to the easy chair. Meanwhile, Clarissa continued her attempts to engage his attention. 'How extraordinary it is,' she observed. 'All my life nothing has really happened to me, and tonight I've had the lot. Murder, police, drug addicts, invisible ink, secret writing, almost arrested for manslaughter, and very nearly murdered.' She paused and looked at Henry. 'You know, darling, in a way it's almost too much all in one evening.'

'Do go and make that coffee, darling,' Henry replied. 'You can tell me all your lovely rigmarole tomorrow.'

Clarissa looked exasperated. 'But don't you realize, Henry,' she asked him, 'that I was nearly murdered this evening?'

Henry looked at his watch. 'Either Sir John or Mr Jones might arrive at any minute,' he said anxiously.

'What I've been through this evening,' Clarissa continued. 'Oh dear, it reminds me of Sir Walter Scott.'

'What does?' Henry asked vaguely as he looked around the room to make sure that everything was now in its proper place.

'My aunt made me learn it by heart,' Clarissa recalled.

Henry looked at her questioningly, and she recited, 'O what a tangled web we weave, when first we practise to deceive.'

Suddenly conscious of her, Henry leaned over the armchair and put his arms around her. 'My adorable spider!' he said.

Clarissa put her arms around his shoulders. 'Do you know the facts of life about spiders?' she asked him. 'They eat their husbands.' She scratched his neck with her fingers.

'I'm more likely to eat you,' Henry replied passionately, as he kissed her.

The front door bell suddenly rang. 'Sir John!' gasped Clarissa, starting away from Henry who exclaimed at the same time, 'Mr Jones!'

Clarissa pushed Henry towards the hall door. 'You go out and answer the front door,' she ordered. 'I'll put coffee and sandwiches in the hall, and you can bring them in here when you're ready for them. High level talks will now begin.' She kissed her hand, then put it to his mouth. 'Good luck, darling.'

'Good luck,' Henry replied. He turned away, then turned back again. 'I mean, thanks. I wonder which one of them has got here first.' Hastily buttoning his jacket and straightening his tie, he rushed off to the front door.

Clarissa picked up the plate and dish, began to go to the hall door, but stopped when she heard Henry's voice saying heartily,

'Good evening, Sir John.' She hesitated briefly, then quickly went over to the bookshelves and activated the panel switch. The panel opened, and she backed into it. 'Exit Clarissa mysteriously,' she declaimed in a dramatic stage whisper as she disappeared into the recess, a split second before Henry ushered the Prime Minister into the drawing-room.

THE PLAYS OF
AGATHA CHRISTIE

Alibi, the earliest Agatha Christie play to reach the stage, opening at the Prince of Wales Theatre, London, in May 1928, was not written by Christie herself. It was an adaptation by Michael Morton of her 1926 crime novel, *The Murder of Roger Ackroyd*, and Hercule Poirot was played by Charles Laughton. Christie disliked both the play and Laughton's performance. It was largely because of her dissatisfaction with *Alibi* that she decided to put Poirot on the stage in a play of her own. The result was *Black Coffee*, which ran for several months at St Martin's Theatre, London, in 1930.

Seven years passed before Agatha Christie wrote her next play, *Akhnaton*. It was not a murder mystery but the story of the ancient Pharaoh who attempted to persuade a polytheistic Egypt to turn to the worship of one deity, the sun-god Aton. *Akhnaton* failed to reach the stage in 1937, and lay forgotten for thirty-five years until, in the course of spring cleaning, its author found the typescript again and had it published.

Although she had disliked *Alibi* in 1928,

Agatha Christie gave her permission, over the years, for five more of her works to be adapted for the stage by other hands. The earliest of these was *Love From a Stranger* (1936), which Frank Vosper, a popular leading man in British theatre in the twenties and thirties, adapted from the short story 'Philomel Cottage', writing the leading male role for himself to play. The 1932 Hercule Poirot novel, *Peril at End House*, became a play of the same title in 1940, adapted by Arnold Ridley, who was well known as the author of *The Ghost Train*, a popular play of the time. With *Murder at the Vicarage*, a 1949 dramatization by Moie Charles and Barbara Toy of a 1940 novel of the same title, Agatha Christie's other popular investigator, Miss Marple, made her stage debut.

Disillusioned with one or two of these stage adaptations by other writers, in 1945 Agatha Christie had herself begun to adapt some of her already published novels for the theatre. The 1939 murder mystery *Ten Little Niggers* (a title later changed, for obvious reasons, to *And Then There Were None*) was staged very successfully both in London in 1943 and in New York the following year.

Christie's adaptation of *Appointment with Death*, a crime novel published in 1928, was staged in 1945, and two other novels which she subsequently turned into plays were *Death on the Nile* (1937), performed in 1945 as *Murder on the Nile*, and *The Hollow*, published in 1946 and staged in 1951. These three novels all featured Hercule Poirot as the investigator, but in adapting them for the stage, Christie removed Poirot. 'I had got used to having Poirot in my books,' she said of one of them, 'and so naturally he had come into this one, but he was all wrong there. He did his stuff all right, but how much better, I kept thinking, would the book have been without him. So when I came to sketch out the play, out went Poirot.'

For her next play after *The Hollow*, Agatha Christie turned not to a novel, but to her short story 'Three Blind Mice', which had itself been based on a radio play she wrote in 1947 for one of her greatest fans, Queen Mary, widow of the British monarch George V. The Queen, who was celebrating her eightieth birthday that year, had asked the BBC to commission a radio play from Agatha Christie, and 'Three Blind Mice' was the result. For its transmogrification into a stage play, a new title was found, lifted from Shakespeare's *Hamlet*. During the performance which Hamlet causes to be staged before Claudius and Gertrude, the King asks, 'What do you call the play?' to which Hamlet replies, 'The Mousetrap'. *The Mousetrap* opened in London in November 1952, and its producer, Peter Saunders, told Christie that he had hopes for a long run of a year or even fourteen months. 'It won't run that long,' the playwright replied. 'Eight months, perhaps.' Fifty years later, *The Mousetrap* is still running, and may well go on for ever.

A few weeks into the run of *The Mousetrap*, Saunders suggested to Agatha Christie that she should adapt for the stage another of her short stories, 'Witness for the Prosecution'. But she thought this would prove too difficult, and told Saunders to try it himself. This he proceeded to do, and in due course he delivered the first draft of a play to her. When she had read it, Christie told him she did not think his version good enough, but that he had certainly shown her how it could be done. Six weeks later, she had completed the play that she later considered one of her best. On its first night in October 1953 at the Winter Garden Theatre in Drury Lane, the audience sat spellbound by the ingenuity of the surprise ending. *Witness for the Prosecution* played for 468 performances, and enjoyed an even longer run of 646 performances in New York.

Shortly after *Witness for the Prosecution* was launched, Agatha Christie agreed to write a play for the British film star, Margaret Lockwood, who wanted a role that would exploit her talent for comedy. The result was an enjoyable comedy-thriller, *Spider's Web*, which made satirical use of that creaky old device, the secret passage. In December 1954, it opened at the Savoy Theatre, where it stayed for 774 performances, joining *The Mousetrap* and *Witness for the Prosecution*. Agatha Christie had three successful plays running simultaneously in London.

For the next theatre venture, Christie collaborated with Gerald Verner to adapt *Towards Zero*, a murder mystery she had written ten years previously. Opening at St James's Theatre in September 1956, it had a respectable run of six months. The author was now in her late sixties, but still producing at least one novel a year and several short stories, as well as working on her autobiography. She was to write five more plays, all but one of them original works for the stage and not adaptations of novels. The exception was *Go Back for Murder*, a stage version of her 1943 Hercule Poirot murder mystery, *Five Little Pigs*, and once again she banished Poirot from the plot, making the investigator a personable young solicitor. The play opened at the Duchess Theatre in March 1960, but closed after only thirty-one performances.

Her four remaining plays, all original stage works, were *Verdict, The Unexpected Guest* (both first staged in 1958), *Rule of Three* (1962), and *Fiddlers Three* (1972). *Rule of Three* is actually three unconnected one-act plays, the last of which, 'The Patient', is an excellent mystery thriller with an unbeatable final line. However, audiences stayed away from this evening of three separate plays, and *Rule of Three* closed at the Duchess Theatre after ten weeks.

Christie's final work for the theatre, *Fiddlers Three*, did not even reach London. It toured the English provinces in 1971 as *Fiddlers Five*, was withdrawn to be rewritten, and reopened at the Yvonne Arnaud Theatre, Guildford, in August 1972. After touring quite successfully for several weeks, it failed to find a suitable London theatre and closed out-of-town.

Verdict, which opened at London's Strand Theatre in May 1958, is unusual in that, although a murder does occur in the play, there is no mystery attached to it, for it is committed in full view of the audience. It closed after a month, but its resilient author murmured, 'At least I am glad *The Times* liked it,' immediately set to work to write another play, and completed it within four weeks. This was *The Unexpected Guest*, which, after a week in Bristol, moved to the

Duchess Theatre, London, where it opened in August 1958 and had a satisfactory run of eighteen months. One of the best of Agatha Christie's plays, its dialogue is taut and effective, and its plot full of surprises, despite being economical and not over-complex. Reviews were uniformly enthusiastic, and now, more than forty years later, it has begun a new lease of life as a novel.

A few months before her death in 1976, Agatha Christie gave her consent for a stage adaptation to be made by Leslie Darbon of her 1950 novel, *A Murder is Announced*, which featured Miss Marple. When the play reached the stage posthumously in 1977, the critic of *The Financial Times* predicted that it would run as long as *The Mousetrap*. It did not.

In 1981, Leslie Darbon adapted one more Christie novel, *Cards on the Table*, a Poirot murder mystery published forty-five years earlier. Taking a leaf from the author's book where Hercule Poirot was concerned, Darbon removed him from the cast of characters. To date, there have been no more stage adaptations of Agatha Christie novels. With *Black Coffee, The Unexpected Guest,* and now *Spider's Web,* I have started a trend in the opposite direction.

CHARLES OSBORNE

Other titles published by Ulverscroft:

BLACK COFFEE

Agatha Christie and Charles Osborne

Fearing for the security of his revolutionary new formula for a powerful explosive, Sir Claud Amory requests the assistance of Hercule Poirot in transferring it safely to the Ministry of Defence. But when the formula disappears from its safe, Amory must change his plans. Locking his house-guests in the library, he informs them that the thief has precisely one minute of darkness in which to return the formula anonymously — or face the great detective even now on his way. The lights go off; by the time they come on again, Amory is dead in his arm-chair . . .

DESTINATION UNKNOWN

Agatha Christie

When a number of leading scientists disappear without trace, concern grows within the international intelligence community — and the one woman who appears to hold the key to the mystery is dying from injuries sustained in a plane crash. Meanwhile, in a Casablanca hotel room, Hilary Craven prepares to take her own life. But her suicide attempt is about to be interrupted by a man who will offer her an altogether more thrilling way to die . . .

THEY CAME TO BAGHDAD

Agatha Christie

Baghdad is holding a secret superpower summit, but the word is out, and an underground organisation in the Middle East is plotting to sabotage the talks. Into this explosive situation appears Victoria Jones, a girl with a yearning for adventure who gets more than she bargains for when a wounded spy dies in her hotel room. The only man who can save the summit is dead. Can Victoria make sense of his dying words: ' . . . Lucifer . . . Basrah . . . Lefarge . . . '?

CROOKED HOUSE

Agatha Christie

The Leonideses are one big happy family living in a sprawling, ramshackle mansion. That is until the head of the household, Aristide, is murdered with a fatal injection. Suspicion naturally falls on the old man's young widow, fifty years his junior. But the murderer has reckoned without the tenacity of Charles Hayward, fiance of the late millionaire's granddaughter . . .